Deanne sat tensely in the moving car. She watched the darkness speed by. She could hear Matt's shallow breathing from the backseat. She was scared.

When they got to All-Children's, the orderlies whisked Matt upstairs to his room for tests. Deanne and the Gleasons nervously paced the hallway. It seemed like a nightmare to Deanne.

Hours before, she had been holding onto Matt in a sun-dappled forest clearing. Now, they were back at the hospital. And Matt was very sick. She swallowed the lump in her throat.

Lurlene McDaniel

IF I SHOULD DIE
BEFORE I WAKE

DARBY CREEK PUBLISHING

This book is dedicated to the memory
of my beloved mother-in-law, Helen.

I would like to thank the following people for their
help and advice in making this book possible. Thanks
to Steve Kasser, Eugenia Kelly, Pat Jacobs, and
Deanah Soto.

Cataloging-in-Publication

McDaniel, Lurlene.
Lurlene McDaniel's If I should die before I wake.
ISBN 1-58196-009-3
          p. ; cm.
Summary: Fourteen-year-old Deanne is not cut out to be the socialite her mother wants
her to be. Instead she becomes a VolunTeen at the children's hospital where her father
works, eventually working on the oncology floor, helping kids with cancer deal with
their illness. But, when one of her patients dies, can she continue?
1. Teenagers—Juvenile fiction. 2. Volunteers—Juvenile fiction. 3. Friendship—
Juvenile fiction. 4. Cancer—Patients—Juvenile fiction. 5. Teenagers and death—
Juvenile fiction. [1. Teenagers—Fiction. 2. Volunteers—Fiction. 3. Friendship—
Fiction. 4. Cancer—Patients—Fiction. 5. Teenagers and death—Fiction.] I. Title. II.
Title: If I should die before I wake.
PZ7.M4784172 If 2004
[Fic] dc22
OCLC: 52907520

Cover photo by Lonnie Duka (Index Stock)
Cover design by Keith Van Norman

Published by Darby Creek Publishing
7858 Industrial Parkway
Plain City, OH 43064
www.darbycreekpublishing.com

Text copyright © 1983 by Lurlene McDaniel

Printed in the United States of America

OPM 15 14 13 12 11 10

1-58196-009-3

One

Deanne paused by the doorway. She heard her mother say her name. *No,* Deanne thought curiously. *She didn't call me. But she did say my name.*

Cautiously, Deanne peeked into the big, sunny kitchen. She could see her mother, Sylvia, standing near her writing desk. She was talking on the phone.

"Oh, Joan," her mother said with a laugh in her voice. "I think that's so kind of you. Of course, Deanne will be thrilled to go with Judson. I can't wait to tell her!"

Deanne felt her stomach lurch and her mouth go dry. *Oh, no! What was her mother promising now?* she wondered to herself. *And with Judson Cortland III?* Deanne knew that the person on the other end of the phone must be Joan Cortland, Judson's mother.

Deanne felt waves of resentment wash over

her. Her mother was at it again. Sylvia Vandervoort was trying to arrange Deanne's life for her once more. *Why can't she just leave me alone?* Deanne thought bitterly. *Why can't she see I'll never be the Star of the Social Register like she is?*

Deanne wanted to run away and hide before her mother saw her standing there. Quickly, Deanne turned back down the hallway, raced through the marbled foyer and up the winding spiral staircase toward her room. She shut her bedroom door with a bang and threw herself across the yellow canopied bed. Hot tears burned in her eyes.

Things always ended this way with Mrs. Vandervoort meddling in her life . . . fixing her up with all the right people . . . making sure she went to all the right places. Why can't she see that I hate and despise all the things the Vandervoort name stands for? Deanne said to herself. That I hate the country club scene Mom so dearly loves? And I can't stand all the meaningless cotillions and parties I'm forced to attend?

Summer was just two months away. Already, Deanne was dreading it. At fourteen, Deanne would be expected to lie around the pool at the country club all summer, while her mother idled away her days playing bridge and golf and discussing Deanne's social future with all the other mothers.

In four more years Deanne would have to face her own coming out party and turn into a *debutante*. It was expected of a Vandervoort. *Why can't my parents be poor?* she wondered. *Why does Dad have to come from such a long line of Pennsylvania aristocrats?*

"Deanne!" Her mother's voice cut through her thoughts like a knife. "Deanne, honey! Come down into the kitchen! I have the most wonderful news for you!"

Deanne wiped her eyes quickly. "C-coming," she called. She didn't want her mother to know she had overheard any of the phone conversation. Deanne looked in the mirror on her vanity. *How plain and pale and fat I look!* she thought.

She tugged her heavy, silver-plated hairbrush through her long, fine, blond hair. On her mother, the same color and texture of hair looked elegant. On Deanne, it looked limp and lifeless. Her pale eyelashes seemed to disappear in her heart-shaped face. And the wool skirt she wore strained at its button around her middle.

"Great!" she said aloud. "Instead of losing weight on this stupid diet, I've gained it."

All in all, Deanne felt she must be a big disappointment to her mother. Here she was, Deanne Vandervoort, the only child of Dr. Hans and Sylvia Vandervoort, a direct descendant of some of the first Dutch settlers in America, a member of the prestigious Social Register, and she hated everything her heritage stood for.

She almost felt sorry for her mother. What bad luck to be stuck with an ugly daughter. Where her mother was tall and slim and pretty, she was short and overweight and not pretty at all. Where her mother was outgoing, witty, and well-liked, she was quiet, introspective and not popular at all. Life just wasn't fair!

"Are you coming?" Sylvia called again.

"Yes!" Deanne answered as she hurried downstairs.

* * * * *

Deanne slouched at the round oak table in the breakfast nook. Her mother beamed at her with excitement. "I just got off the phone with Joan Cortland," she smiled. "Guess what?"

Deanne shrugged her shoulders, afraid to look at her mother's face. She was afraid she would burst into tears.

"Deanne, dear," her mother interrupted herself. "Please sit up straight. Don't slump."

Deanne squared her shoulders. "Guess who's taking you to the Hospital Charity Ball next month?"

Deanne caught her breath.

"Judson Cortland!" Mrs. Vandervoort smiled triumphantly. Deanne felt her cheeks burn hotly. *How could Mother do this to me?* she asked herself. How could she humiliate me by arranging a date with the most handsome boy in the entire city? *The* most popular boy in school!

"Well, you could at least show some enthusiasm," her mother said.

"I don't want to go . . .," Deanne began.

"Not go! You can't be serious!" Mrs. Vandervoort cried. "But Deanne, it's not only *the* social event of the spring season, your own mother is chairperson of the entire event. And your father is chief of staff at All-Children's. Why, you must know how important this ball is!"

Deanne hung her head feeling guilty. Of course, she knew how important the annual Charity Ball was to All-Children's Hospital. Most of the funds to run the hospital came from the ball. With her father as chief of staff, as well as one of the top surgeons on the East

9

Coast, she knew the ball was important to his position, too.

But she hated the circus atmosphere of the entire thing. Why did something as important as raising money to save the lives of sick kids have to depend on a stupid social event like the Charity Ball? Why did her mother have to fix her up with a date for the ball?

Deanne thought she knew the answer to that question: No guy would ever think to ask her out on his own. *Who would want to go out with an overweight frump like me?* she thought.

"It's out of the question," Mrs. Vandervoort said forcefully. "You are going to the ball. We are going shopping for a beautiful new dress for you. And you *will* have a wonderful time with Judson. Is that clear?"

Deanne bit her lower lip hard and nodded. *Mother-1, Deanne-0,* she thought. *As usual.*

Suddenly, Mrs. Vandervoort glanced down at her watch. "Oh, my! Look at the time. I have to be at the hospital in thirty minutes for a Guild meeting about the ball. We have a million details to go over. Go get your sweater, and I'll bring the car around to the front driveway."

Her mother left the large, sunny kitchen and Deanne got up heavily from the table.

Normally, she loved going to the hospital. But now she felt so depressed. Once again she was stuck doing exactly what her mother wanted her to do. *It doesn't matter one bit what I want to do,* she thought.

Deanne looked longingly at the refrigerator. How she would love to sit down with a big bowl of ice cream! But of course, there was no time. And besides, her mother would kill her.

The car horn sounded. Deanne rushed for the hall closet to get a sweater. It would be cool in the late spring afternoon air. She felt lonely and angry. She had to find a way to stop her mother from running her life. She couldn't face a whole summer of arranged dates and boring, empty parties. She refused to spend all her time chasing around after her mother's dreams.

Deanne locked the front door, slamming it behind her.

Judson Cortland III! Deanne felt her cheeks flush. *How could Mother do this to me?* she wondered.

"Really, Deanne, stop overreacting. He's a very nice boy. And very handsome, too, I might add."

"Oh, yes," Deanne agreed, her mind a jumble of thoughts. Yes, Judson was very handsome, all right. He was also the most popular boy at Baylor Prep. She could just imagine the look on his face when his mother broke the news to him about his date for the ball. Deanne swallowed hard and tried to pretend it didn't matter. But it did. Imagine . . . Judson stuck with dull, boring, overweight Deanne Vandervoort. *How humiliating!* she said to herself.

"You shouldn't have done it, Mother," she mumbled beneath her breath.

"Why not?" her mother shrugged. "You'll have a perfectly lovely time, dear. Who knows? Maybe you'll hit it off and have a perfectly wonderful summer together. I know the Cortlands sail a lot. You'd like to spend some time this summer sailing, wouldn't you?"

Deanne just stared out the car window. *Terrific!* she thought. *Now Mother has my entire summer laid out for me. Well, I'm not going to do it!* Deanne thought angrily. *I don't know how yet. But, I'm not going to spend the summer chasing around after Mother's dreams. I'll run away from home first!*

Two

"**D**r. Carter . . . please call the nurses' station, fifth floor," the soft voice of the paging system sounded through the hospital lobby. Deanne paused inside the front door and looked around the spacious, colorful lobby area.

Since it was a children's hospital, the walls were very bright and cheerful. Large cartoon characters adorned two walls off to the right where a sitting area was located. Next to the sitting area was the information desk and then long corridors leading to administrative offices, out-patient care, X-ray and the pharmacy.

To the right of the entrance was the gift shop and a small snack bar, complete with vending machines, and small tables and chairs. Deanne noted that since her last visit to the hospital they installed two video games in the snack bar area, too.

"Now, Deanne, I'm almost late for my Guild meeting," her mother told her hurriedly in the lobby. "I've got to get down to the conference room. So be a dear, and try to locate your father. Let's see . . .," she added, glancing at her watch. "It's four-thirty. He may be up on surgical rounds. Anyway, let him know we're here and that I'll be finished in about an hour and a half. Maybe you can persuade him to take us out to supper."

Deanne nodded, anxious for her mother to be on her way. She wanted to be alone and out from under her mother's eye. Deanne loved the busy atmosphere of the hospital. Everyone was so active and friendly. The nurses seemed so attentive. They always had a smile for her.

Deanne had been too young to have free run of the hospital before, but now that she was fourteen, she could go just about anywhere she pleased. She had spent hours exploring the place . . . from the basement cafeteria to the out-patient clinic to each of the five floors. She knew that the hospital was considered to be one of the best in the country for treating children. It had 250 beds and was filled to capacity much of the year.

It specialized in the treatment of sick kids:

kids with heart problems, kidney problems, infectious diseases, diabetes, and even cancer. The Oncology Department was located on the fourth floor, and she had never done more than glance down the halls. It always made her sad to think about all the kids with cancer.

Deanne stepped off the elevator onto the surgical floor. She knew this floor best of all. This was the area where her father spent most of his time. She approached the central nurses' station and peered over the top of the octagon-shaped desk top.

"Hi," she smiled at an R.N. who was bent over a flip chart.

"Well, hello, Deanne," the nurse said with a smile as she looked up from her chart work. "Looking for your dad?"

"Yes, I am," Deanne said. "Is he still on rounds?"

"I'm not sure," the nurse said. "But, I think his secretary is still in his office if you want to ask her."

"Thanks," Deanne called as she headed down the corridor toward her father's office. The halls were busy. Deanne knew that the dinner cart would soon be up and that the staff was preparing for the visiting hours. Things would probably be hectic from now until about nine o'clock when everything settled down for the night.

Semi-private rooms lined the corridor. Most of the televisions in the rooms were on. Deanne could see kids in their rooms as she walked down the hallway. The young patients were either recovering from surgery or waiting for surgery. The rooms were bright and cheerful, and the equipment was new and sparkling clean.

Deanne turned into the little cubbyhole that was her father's office. His secretary, Carol McGinnis, glanced up from her typewriter. "Well, hey there, Deanne!" the brown-eyed woman called.

Deanne smiled back. "Hi. Is Dad around?"

"Not right now. But I expect him back any minute. Why don't you wait? He shouldn't be long," Carol said.

Deanne slid onto a chair and looked at the wall clock. It was five o'clock and already her stomach was starting to growl. "So, how's the ball coming along?" Carol asked.

For a minute, Deanne had forgotten all about her mother, the ball, and her "date" with Judson. It came back in a painful rush. "Fine," she shrugged. "Are you going?"

"Me?" Carol laughed. "You must be kidding! I don't rub elbows with the country club set."

Neither do I, Deanne thought glumly. But she said, "You should come."

"Hey, I'm a working girl, remember? I can't afford a one-hundred-dollar-a-plate dinner no matter how worthy the cause."

"Carol, . . . any messages?" The deep voice belonged to Dr. Hans Vandervoort. "Deanne!" he smiled. "Let me guess . . . your mother's at a Guild meeting and she sent you up to try and lure me into taking you both out to supper?"

Deanne blushed and laughed out loud. He certainly knew his wife and her habits! "You're right," Deanne said.

"Well, I've got to dictate some notes for Carol to type up tomorrow. So it's going to be about an hour before I'm free."

"Same for Mom," Deanne told him.

"Can you find something to do for an hour?" he said.

Deanne's heart leaped. She'd love to have a whole hour to roam around the hospital by herself. "You bet!" she said.

"Good. Run along then and I'll meet you and Mom at the front entrance at six-fifteen. That should give us both plenty of time to wrap up our business."

Deanne waved good-bye, but Carol was already handing Dr. Vandervoort a stack of

17

phone messages. They didn't notice as she left the office.

Deep in thought, she headed down the corridor toward the elevators. For as long as she could remember, she had adored her father. He was so tall and handsome. His hair was prematurely gray, and his eyes were an electric-blue color. *Why can't Mom be more like him?* she thought. Her dad was busy, too, and he was probably one of the most respected men in the city. But he never seemed to be interested in the social life his wife loved so much.

Hans Vandervoort was a true physician. His great-grandfather had been a doctor. So had his grandfather and his father before him. Yet, he never seemed to mind the demanding hours and the hard work. Deanne had often wondered if he had ever wanted to be anything else. Or, was it just assumed he would be a doctor like every other man in his family?

She wished her father had had more time for her when she was younger. But he was always so busy. Since she was an only child, she was often lonely. But she always understood that a man like her father belonged to his patients and to the world of medicine. Now that she was older, she hoped she could spend more time around him here at the hospital.

The elevator doors slid open on the ground floor. Deanne stepped out and decided to buy herself a soft drink in the snack bar. Maybe a soda would quiet her growling stomach until it was time for supper. Her mother would be very angry if she knew that Deanne bought a bag of chips but she *was* hungry.

"Deanne! Deanne Vandervoort, is that you?" Deanne turned at the sound of her name and saw a girl coming toward her from across the lobby. It was a girl from her science class.

"Susan Pyle?" Deanne asked.

"Hi," the blue-eyed, blond-haired girl beamed. "I thought that was you."

For the first time, Deanne noticed Susan's clothes. She was dressed in a cherry-red smock over a white blouse and white slacks. She looked crisp and clean and very professional. "What are you doing here?" Deanne asked, her curiosity spilling over into her voice.

"Oh, I'm a VolunTeen," Susan answered.

"You work here?" Deanne asked, surprised.

"Volunteer work," Susan said. "It's only two days a week after school and one Saturday a month. I can't wait until summer. Then, I'm going to be here a lot more."

"You're kidding?" Deanne couldn't believe it.

She remembered Susan as a quiet girl who kept mostly to herself at school.

"Oh, it's really fun!" Susan told her. "Besides, I never could get into all those dumb clubs and things at school."

Deanne knew what she meant. "Well, what do you do?" she asked.

"Anything they need me to do. Sometimes I help in the gift shop. Sometimes I play with some of the little kids in the rec room. Or, I help the nurses feed the babies their lunch on Saturday. Right now, I'm waiting to take someone up from admissions who's just checking into the hospital. Gee," Susan paused, "with your father a doctor and all, I thought you'd know all about the VolunTeen program."

Deanne blushed. She was ashamed to admit she didn't know much about it. She knew that the hospital depended heavily on its volunteer staff. But she never dreamed that fourteen-year-old kids could be a part of the program.

"It's a great place to work," Susan continued. "And the nurses are super—except for Mrs. Sanders. Wow! What a dragon," Susan confided, her eyes wide.

Deanne sorted through her memory for Mrs. Sanders. Then she remembered her. She was head nurse in charge of the All-Children's nursing staff. Deanne didn't know her personally.

"Oops," Susan said as an older woman wearing a cherry-colored smock like Susan's signaled to her from the Admission's Office doorway. "Gotta run now. Nice to see you."

Deanne watched as Susan hurried inside the office. Susan emerged a few minutes later, pushing a wheelchair. In the chair sat a boy of about sixteen. He looked thin, but he was also really good-looking. He had thick, brown hair and a square-cut jaw. A small, black suitcase and a duffle bag were balanced across his lap.

"I can walk, you know," he grumbled at Susan.

"I'm sure you can," Susan said. "But it's hospital policy. Everyone who checks in gets a ride in a wheelchair. Besides, you don't want me out of a job, do you?"

Before he could answer, a cluster of people came out of admissions after him. Deanne could hardly believe her eyes. The man and woman had to be the boy's parents. And there were four girls and one little boy who had to be his sisters and brother. The family resemblance was unmistakable. Six kids in one family! Deanne just stood and stared.

"Now, honey, you know Dad and I'll be back just as soon as we get the kids fed and settled down," the small, dark-haired woman told the boy in the chair. Her face was lined with worry.

"Hey, Mom," the boy said softly. "It's all right. I'll be fine." He reached out and held her hand.

"Son . . .," the boy's father said. His voice cracked slightly. He couldn't go on talking.

"Look," the boy said. "Go on. This beautiful lady is going to give me a ride to my room and by the time I get it all together, you'll both be back."

Susan smiled self-consciously. Then, one by one, the kids lined up and kissed their brother. They all seemed so sad!

Suddenly, Deanne blushed. She realized she had been standing there, staring at the entire scene like a dope. She felt like an eavesdropper. Slowly, she backed away from the scene. She wished she could drop through the floor.

Susan pushed the wheelchair into the open elevator and the family group watched the doors close. Then they all turned and started for the outside doors. They had to pass

Deanne. Their steps seemed heavy and slow. Their faces were sad and worried.

Deanne felt very small and foolish. *Here were people with REAL problems,* she thought sadly. Somehow Deanne's problems didn't seem so big after all. She wondered what was wrong with the boy. And her heart went out to these perfect strangers.

Three

Deanne was running late. She knew that her mother would be waiting for her at the big circular driveway in front of Baylor Prep's entrance. She'd be gunning her engine and glancing at her watch. *Well, too bad!* Deanne thought angrily. *You can just wait.*

She looked around the empty classroom to make sure everything was in order. Since she was one of the top students in Mr. Rose's geometry class, Deanne had special privileges to grade test papers for the lower classes. Mr. Rose had left about fifteen minutes before. "Are you sure you don't mind finishing up?" Mr. Rose had asked.

"Oh, no," Deanne had said.

"Thanks, Deanne. I wish I had more students like you. Listen, just flip off the lights when you're done," Mr. Rose had said.

She had smiled and had finished her work

in the quiet of the empty room and deserted halls. Almost everyone had gone home by now.

Mrs. Vandervoort had told Deanne that morning that there was a Guild meeting at the hospital and that she would be late picking Deanne up from school. With the ball only three days away, Deanne barely saw her mother. It seemed her mother was busy day and night.

Deanne flipped off the light switch and stepped into the hallway. There was no one to be seen. Her heels clicked on the wooden floors as she hurried toward the front entrance where her mother would be waiting. Suddenly, she heard voices. The voices were coming from around the corner next to the front entrance.

She stopped. Her heart pounded. She heard her name spoken. Two male voices were coming from around the corner. And they were talking about HER!

"That's too bad, man," the first voice said.

"Yeah, I know. What a drag," the second voice added. "I gotta waste a whole Saturday at the dumb Charity Ball with Deanne Vandervoort. Ugh!"

Deanne slapped her hand over her mouth. The second voice was Judson's! Her cheeks flushed and she tried to hold her breath.

"At least she's smart," the first voice said.

"Terrific!" Judson muttered. "We can sit around all night and compare math notes."

"What's Mindy saying?"

Deanne knew they meant Mindy Fryer, one of the prettiest girls in school.

"She's upset. But my mom arranged it and now I'm stuck."

Deanne felt tears spring to her eyes. So that's how he felt about a date with her!

"Too bad," said the first voice. "Well, if you need me to take Mindy off your hands for Saturday night . . ."

"Forget it! Mindy's my problem. You keep your hands off."

Their voices faded down the hall and Deanne leaned weakly against the wall. She felt humiliated and then angry. "I hate you, Judson Cortland!" she said under her breath. "I wish I didn't have to see you ever again!"

Suddenly, she remembered that her mother was waiting in the car. Deanne felt angry at her, too. *How could you do this to me?* she thought. She vowed that she would do anything to get away from her mother's plans for her that summer. Anything!

* * * * *

26

Everything about the ball was beautiful. Everything except the way Deanne felt inside. She had never been more miserable. The country club was elegantly decorated. There was a large, richly-dressed crowd of people. The orchestra played, people danced, speakers gave speeches, and door prizes were auctioned off. Everyone was having a wonderful time, except Deanne.

Deanne and Judson barely spoke during the evening. She couldn't stand to even look at him. After all, she knew how he *really* felt about her. She only saw her parents from across the room. Her mother was busy and everyone was making such a fuss over her and her "most successful ball ever." Deanne could only think about her own misery. She couldn't wait to go home and peel the forced smile off her face and go to bed and cry.

She excused herself from the table for the twentieth time and headed for the ladies room. Judson ignored her. The floor was crowded and she had to walk along the wall to get out of the room.

To her left, she noticed a special table. It was tagged with a large red heart that read: "Our Volunteers—True Angels." Then she heard someone calling her name from the table.

"Deanne! Deanne! Over here!"

"Susan!" Deanne cried. She hurried over to Susan's table. It was good to see a friendly face.

"I figured you'd be here. Isn't it fabulous?" Susan's eyes shined.

Deanne dropped into the chair next to Susan. "It's okay," she said. Then she added, "I didn't know you were coming."

"Oh, yeah. They always have a special table for the volunteers. Mostly the older volunteers come, but this year some of the VolunTeens got to come, too. I'm having a great time! Do you have a date?"

Deanne lowered her eyes. She hoped Susan wouldn't see the pain in them. "Sort of . . . Judson Cortland. I came with him and his parents."

"Wow!" Susan said. "He's neat."

Deanne quickly changed the subject. "So you really like being a VolunTeen, huh?"

"It's the most fun in the world!" Susan sounded excited. "I can't wait until summer when I can work more hours."

"How do you get to be one?" Deanne asked.

"You just apply to Pat Jacobson. She's the director of the program at All-Children's. She interviews you, checks your grades, then sends you through orientation if she thinks you can hack it. Next thing you know," Susan snapped her fingers, "you're working up on the floors with the nurses and kids. I think I might become a nurse or doctor someday."

Deanne leaned back in her chair and appraised Susan. There was nothing special about her. She was nice, yet ordinary. But Deanne felt jealous. They were the same age and both made good grades. They were even in the same school. But Susan was happy and involved and full of vitality. The only difference Deanne could see was that Susan was a part of the VolunTeen program and she wasn't.

The wheels began to spin in her mind.

* * * * *

"You want to do WHAT this summer?" her mother asked, raising her voice and setting her coffee cup down with a thump.

Deanne tossed her head and sat on her hands at the dining table to keep them from shaking. "You heard me," Deanne said in a braver voice than she felt. "I want to be a VolunTeen at the hospital."

"Why, that's silly," her mother said with a wave of dismissal.

"It is not!" Deanne shot back. "I talked to

29

this girl at my school and she's a VolunTeen. And she loves it!"

"Well, what possible reason could a young girl like you have for wanting to be hidden away inside that old hospital with a bunch of sick children?" Mrs. Vandervoort asked.

"Dad is!" Deanne said. She looked over at her father. He put down his newspaper to listen to his wife and daughter.

Deanne was hoping he'd be on her side. She looked over at him with a silent appeal for help.

"Now, wait a minute, Sylvia," he rumbled in his deep, commanding voice. "I spend all of my time 'hidden away with a bunch of sick kids.'"

"That's different, Hans. It's your job," said Mrs. Vandervoort.

"Exactly Deanne's point," he said. "A volunteer position is kind of like a job. We couldn't run the place without our volunteers. You should know that," Dr. Vandervoort said.

Deanne kept quiet. She would let her father fight some for her. "But Deanne's just fourteen," her mother added. "She doesn't need to think about a job. Besides, there are too many fun things for a girl her age to be doing all summer. She should be meeting other girls her age."

"But, Mom," Deanne blurted out, "I really want to be a VolunTeen. I-I've already talked to Pat Jacobson."

"Without my permission?" her mother asked.

"It shows spunk," Dr. Vandervoort interjected. "It shows how much she wants to do it."

"Mrs. Jacobson said that I would make a good VolunTeen. I just have to go through orientation."

"I won't pull strings for you, Deanne," her father said sternly.

"I won't ask you to," Deanne told him. "Honest. I'll be on my own. I'll do a good job . . . I promise!"

"Sounds fair enough to me."

"Now, just a minute, you two!" Mrs. Vandervort said. "You talk as if it's a fact. I haven't agreed."

"I'll have time for other things," Deanne said eagerly. "The orientation is a week from Saturday. I can only work a few hours a week at the start anyway."

"But how would you get there and back?" Mrs. Vandervoort asked, looking for a weakness in the plan.

"I'll ride back and forth with Dad," Deanne

finished. She could sense her victory.

"I don't know . . .," her mother said with a scowl. "If he runs late, I'll have to come and pick you up, I'm sure."

"Oh, let Deanne give it a try," Dr. Vandervoort said. "If she sticks with it, fine. If not, she can drop out."

"I WILL stick with it, Dad," Deanne said firmly.

"I'm sure you will," he said with a wink. "After all, you ARE a Vandervoort."

"Oh!" Mrs. Vandervoort said loudly. "All right. Do whatever you want. But, don't blame me when your whole summer has gone by and you've had no fun."

Deanne jumped up from the table. "Thanks, Dad . . . and Mom," she added. "Can I ride into the hospital this morning? I want to tell Mrs. Jacobson and get on the orientation list."

"Sure," he said. "You've got fifteen minutes to be ready. One lesson you'll learn first. Don't ever be late, and don't ever keep me waiting."

"You got it!" Deanne cried, running from the dining room and up the winding staircase toward her bedroom. Her heart was pounding. She won! She'd actually gotten her way with her mother!

Suddenly, her stomach gave a little flutter. Now what? Could she really do the job? Would she love it like Susan does? She'd won . . . but what if she hated it? "I'll have to make it work," she said aloud in her room. She was finally out from under her mother's thumb. She was going to make the most of it.

Four

Deanne would have never made it through the first week if it hadn't been for Susan. She helped her do everything. She was patient and helpful and the best friend Deanne ever had. Deanne's biggest problem was her fear of making a mistake.

That was really all Mrs. Sanders's fault. Every scary story Deanne had ever heard about the head nurse was true. On the first day of orientation, Mrs. Sanders had spoken to the eager new VolunTeens. The girls listened with their fullest attention. When Mrs. Sanders spoke, *everyone* listened.

Hope I never meet her in a dark hallway, Deanne had thought to herself. But after the program had broken for lunch, she saw Mrs. Sanders marching toward her.

"So you're Miss Vandervoort?" Mrs. Sanders had asked in a voice as crisp and starched as her uniform.

"Y-yes," Deanne mumbled. Her heart pounded.

"I want you to understand something," Mrs. Sanders said, her brows furrowed. "Just because your father's chief of staff at this hospital does not mean that you will receive any special treatment."

Deanne was speechless.

"I will expect you to work just as hard as any other VolunTeen around here. My nurses need good help."

Deanne could only tremble and nod. Mrs. Sanders turned to walk away. She stopped, turned back, and added, "In fact, because your father is a doctor, I expect you to work even harder. You already know the type of dedication to medicine it takes to run a good hospital. The only thing we care about is our patients. We are here to serve them. Do you understand?" Deanne nodded again.

"Fine," Mrs. Sanders said curtly. Then she walked away. Deanne lived in mortal fear of her from that day forward.

"Don't let her get to you," Susan had consoled her afterward. "She's tough . . . but you'll find you'll want to please her more than anything."

Deanne had her doubts. She would just try

to stay out of Mrs. Sanders's way.

* * * * *

Deanne settled into the hospital's routine. The days she had duty, she and Susan would report to the nursing stations on each floor and get their assignments. They did everything from changing beds to changing babies, from writing letters for kids with broken limbs to reading to little kids too sick to go to the rec rooms for the Child-Life Program.

Deanne liked working with the Child-Life Specialist, Clare Coffman, best of all. Twice a day the VolunTeens were responsible for getting kids into the rec rooms for playtime. They played games, worked puzzles, baked cookies, drew pictures, and made crafts.

They'd bring the kids down in wheelchairs and work with them for a couple of hours and then take them back to their rooms. The groups were divided into age categories. Deanne loved working with the two- to five-year-old children most. They were cute. As an only child, Deanne had never been around little kids before. She discovered that she liked them.

She also helped in the gift shop, with the bookmobile, and with the New Patient

Orientation Program. She would take kids up and down the elevators for special tests and X rays. She even pushed them in their wheelchairs outside and around the grounds in the warm summer air.

The days passed quickly and soon Deanne found herself spending more and more time at the hospital, working. She and Susan became the favorite team with most of the nursing staff.

Deanne had favorites of her own on the staff.

One afternoon, after her shift was over, Deanne hurried to her father's office. She was running a little late. But she didn't want to keep him waiting.

"Sorry, Deanne," Mrs. McGinnis, his secretary said. "He's still in surgery."

Deanne caught her breath and then wandered down the hall. She drifted into the small rec room on the surgery floor. Books, games, toys, and puzzles lay all over the child-sized tables, the floor and the messy bookshelves. She sat down with a tired sigh.

"I'm whipped," she told herself from the hardness of the wooden yellow chair.

"Well, what are you doing?" a voice snapped behind her. "Waiting for the stuff to put itself away?"

Deanne turned so sharply that she fell off the chair. She turned red as she looked up into the stern face of Mrs. Sanders. "Well . . . I . . . that is . . . I mean," Deanne sputtered.

"Get to work, girl!" Mrs. Sanders commanded.

"B-but . . . I'm off . . .," Deanne began and then wished she could have eaten her own words.

"So what?" Mrs. Sanders snapped back. "We can't wait until you're 'on' again for this mess to get cleaned up, now, can we?"

"No . . . no," Deanne said, scurrying around on all fours, scooping up puzzle pieces.

"Honestly, you girls think your duty is restricted to the hours you work! This is a hospital and we all work until everything is done. Is that clear?"

"Yes, Mrs. Sanders," Deanne gulped.

She looked up to find herself alone. Mrs. Sanders had stalked off. Deanne felt tears stinging her eyes. *How dare she yell at me!* she thought hotly. *I work hard for this place.*

Mrs. Sanders sounded just like her mother in many ways. Oh, the words were different, but the tone was the same. It's not fair! she muttered to herself. Deanne had taken this job to get away from her bossy mother. Now, all of a sudden, she had a bossy boss!

Deanne's mouth set firmly while she cleaned up the room. Well, she'd show them all! She was going to be the best VolunTeen All-Children's ever had. She didn't care what they made her do!

* * * * *

"Miss Vandervoort! Corners on a hospital bed must be sharp and neat!" Deanne pulled back from the edge of the bed she was struggling to make.

"Like this, Miss Vandervoort," Mrs. Sanders said, stepping next to Deanne and expertly folding the fresh linen into place.

"Yes, Mrs. Sanders," Deanne mumbled.

"Now, let me watch you do it," said Mrs. Sanders as she moved to the foot of the bed.

Deanne felt her blood boil. She'd show the old biddy! Her fingers flew and she folded the next corner perfectly.

"Better, Miss Vandervoort," Mrs. Sanders said. "Better."

It went like that every day. No matter what Deanne did, Mrs. Sanders was around to tell her how to do it better. Finally, Susan asked, "Has she got something against you?"

"I think so," Deanne sighed. The two girls

sat in the cafeteria, sipping soft drinks during a break. "I think she doesn't like the fact that I'm a doctor's daughter," Deanne continued.

"So what?" Susan asked.

"I think she feels she should push me harder. Plus, I don't think she likes me very much," Deanne confided.

"Gee, that's too bad. Too bad she's in charge of all the nurses. That means she's all over the hospital," Susan said.

"Not too much up on oncology," Deanne told Susan. "I asked my dad. He said that oncology has its own special staff, special programs, and special needs. She doesn't haunt the halls too much up there. But then, neither do we," Deanne added.

"Some of the VolunTeens do," Susan mused. "I wonder what it's like? And I wonder how you get picked for that duty?"

"I don't think I'd like it," Deanne said. "It seems so depressing. Kids with cancer . . . ugh!"

"But, they're still kids," Susan reminded her.

* * * * *

"Honey, I do believe you're losing weight." Mrs. Vandervoort appraised her daughter with a critical eye. Deanne put on lipstick in front of her bedroom mirror.

"Oh, yeah . . . a few pounds," Deanne admitted casually. She had lost five pounds since she started working. She already had to move buttons over on the pants of her uniform. And the white blouse looked a lot less snug than when she first put it on three weeks before. Frankly, she was too busy to think about eating. She rarely took time to eat more than a container of yogurt for lunch. By the time she got home, she was too tired to eat much dinner.

"Well, then this job's been good for you," her mother said. "But you sure haven't been getting out to the country club like you said you would."

Deanne rolled her eyes. "I'm just too busy."

"Joan Cortland asked about you the other day," Mrs. Vandervoort began.

Deanne froze. The last person in the world she wanted to hear about was Judson Cortland.

"I'm disappointed that you and Judson aren't seeing more of each other. I mean, he's such a nice young man. The Cortlands sail a lot, you know. We could join them at their beach place any weekend we want—"

"Oops!" Deanne said, looking at her watch. "Can't talk now, Mother. Dad will be honking his horn for me any minute now! You know how he hates to be kept waiting!"

"But, Deanne, I'm not finished!" her mother called after Deanne as she ran down the stairs from her room.

"Later, Mother!" Deanne called up. "Much later!" she added under her breath. She promised herself that she would increase her volunteer hours at the hospital that very day. She was going to stay as busy as she possibly could—even if it meant being under the eye of Mrs. Sanders twice as much!

Five

The wheel on the bookmobile was stuck. "Rats!" Deanne muttered as she struggled with the uncooperative cart. Her arms ached from fighting with the thing. She wasn't even half finished with her rounds on the third floor.

"Come on, cart!" she said aloud. "Have some consideration." But the large portable cart stopped short as its wheels refused to turn.

"Problems?" Deanne heard Mrs. Sanders ask from behind her.

"No," Deanne answered, a little too quickly. "It's just being stubborn."

"Let me see," Mrs. Sanders said, taking over the bar handle of the cart. With effortless motion the cart slid forward. Deanne only stared in disbelief. "Seems to be working fine, now," Mrs. Sanders said with a sniff.

"I guess you have the magic touch," Deanne mumbled weakly. She glared at the cart as Mrs. Sanders continued crisply down the hall.

Deanne got it into a room. Sara Miller smiled broadly as Deanne came through the door. "Hi, Miss Deanne!" the little girl grinned from her hospital bed.

"Good afternoon, Sara. Need a book today?"

"What ya got?" the child asked.

"Want a good mystery? Or, how about a horse story?" She handed Sara a green-covered book about horses.

"Yeah!" Sara smiled. "I love horse stories." Deanne filled out the patient's name and the book title on her information chart.

"You gonna be down at the rec room for arts and crafts?" Sara asked.

Deanne checked her watch. Oh, my goodness . . . it's less than an hour from now. I'm not even half finished with my bookmobile rounds, she said to herself. "Of course I am, Sara. Let me get rolling here and I'll be back for you in an hour."

Deanne tugged the cart out the door and back into the hall. The wheel stuck again. "Drat!" she said. Then she gave it one big push in disgust.

The wheel released, suddenly. The bookmobile leaped out of her hands. Deanne watched in horror as it swung around crazily, careened toward the wall and hit with a sharp THUMP! Books flew everywhere! Nurses came running. Kids came to the doors of their rooms to see what had happened.

"Oh, no!" Deanne cried. She scrambled to pick up the books.

"Now what happened?" Deanne looked up from the floor into Mrs. Sanders's face.

"It got stuck," Deanne said weakly.

"Miss Vandervoort," Mrs. Sanders began. "I always seem to be looking at you on your hands and knees." She tapped her toe as she spoke. "If the bookmobile is giving you a problem, may I suggest you call a custodian. He would gladly oil the wheels for you, and you could be about your business with fewer mishaps."

"Yes, Mrs. Sanders," Deanne nodded. "I'm sorry."

Mrs. Sanders only looked down her nose and sighed.

* * * * *

Clare Coffman, the Child-Life Program specialist, showed the eager group of children how to fold, cut, and paste a colorful tissue paper flower. Deanne, Susan, and two other VolunTeens, Kathy and Chris, watched closely. They would have to help the kids make the flowers during the two-hour recreation period. Since this was the favorite part of Deanne's day, she found it easy to pay attention.

"That's it, kids," Clare smiled broadly. "Now, have a go at it." The kids all began talking and working at once.

Deanne hurried from child to child, supervising the activity. "Nice job, Kenny. Wait, Alan, I think you're supposed to fold it like this first. That's right, Sara, you've got it." she said. The time flew. She couldn't believe that two hours had gone by when Clare called a halt to the work.

The VolunTeens wheeled the patients back to their rooms. Then they returned and began to clean up the scraps of paper and sticky paste messes.

"Thanks a lot, girls," Clare said to the four helpers.

"It was fun," Deanne told her.

"I wish they all had your attitude, Deanne," Clare said. "You're the best help I have."

Deanne blushed. Then she said, "Tell Mrs. Sanders. She thinks I'm Klutz of the Year."

Clare looked over at her. "Oh, but I have told Mrs. Sanders," she said.

Deanne almost dropped her cleaning sponge. "What?" she gasped. The other girls listened intently.

Clare threw back her head and laughed. "Oh, honestly . . . don't act so shocked. Whenever I have good help, I let people know. You do a fine job. Plus, you really seem to like doing it."

"Oh, I do," Deanne said. "It's . . . oh, you know . . . Mrs. Sanders sees me falling all over myself so much. How's she going to believe you?"

"It's been my experience, Deanne, that Mrs. Sanders only pushes the ones she thinks are good. Believe me, it would be worse if she just ignored you."

"HA!" Deanne scoffed.

"I mean it," Clare continued. "We need sensitive, caring volunteers. These kids need people who can make them feel less scared—people who can relate to them. You're lucky because you can."

After Clare left the room, Deanne thought about what she had said. She really did care. She loved her job and she liked the people she worked with.

"Well, that's it for me," Kathy said, pushing her hands against her back. "I'm going downstairs for lunch."

"Yeah," Chris and Susan agreed. "But why don't we sit for a minute first," Susan sighed. "My feet are killing me!"

They all plopped onto the floor and stretched out. It felt good to relax. "Just think," Deanne piped up. "We get to do it all over again in two hours." The other three girls groaned.

"Haven't you girls got anything to do?" the voice from the doorway asked. It was Mrs. Sanders. The girls jumped to their feet.

"Oh, sure!" Kathy said. "Lunch, you know."

"Fine," Mrs. Sanders said. "Then get to it. We'll be needing some of you to strip and change beds this afternoon."

They all nodded and headed toward the door. Each wanted a fast escape to the cafeteria. "Just a minute," Mrs. Sanders called. "Miss Vandervoort, I'd like to speak with you for a minute."

Deanne froze in her steps. Her heart skipped a beat. "Yes, Mrs. Sanders?" she asked, turning toward the stern-faced nurse.

"I want to give you a special assignment. You too, Miss Pyle." Susan stopped next to Deanne.

"Yes, Mrs. Sanders?" she also asked.

The other girls left the room in a hurry. Deanne and Susan waited for Mrs. Sanders to speak. Finally, she said, "I've gotten some good reports about you two girls, about your hard work and initiative."

They waited for her to continue. "They're short-handed upstairs in oncology. The ChildLife Program there needs some volunteers." She stared at them until they each nodded.

"As you know, these cancer patients have their own recreation areas. We need VolunTeens to help out and I'm personally sending you two up there. You'll report to Renee Stewart. She's the R.N. in charge during the day shift. She'll tell you what she needs you to do."

Deanne and Susan stood and stared at Mrs. Sanders.

"Did you hear me?" Mrs. Sanders asked.

"Yes, Mrs. Sanders!" they chimed in unison.

"Then get moving, please," Mrs. Sanders said as she turned to leave.

The girls dashed for the elevators and pushed the button for the fourth floor. Deanne's heart was pounding. She didn't like this one bit. She felt nervous about being around kids with cancer. And she didn't like Mrs. Sanders "volunteering" her to do it.

* * * * *

The oncology floor looked like every other floor of the hospital: a central nurses' station, rows of rooms, and a large rec room at the end of the hall. The first person Deanne saw when she got off the elevator was a ten-year-old boy. He was very thin, and he was pushing a portable IV stand. Two bags of IV solution hung from either side of the stand. Long, clear plastic tubes ran from the bottles to the needle in the back of his hand. Deanne turned her head and walked quickly to the nurses' station.

"Mrs. Stewart?" she asked. A green-eyed woman dressed in crisp white looked up.

"Yes?" she asked.

"We're the VolunTeens Mrs. Sanders sent up," Deanne continued.

Renee Stewart smiled. "Good, I've been waiting for you." As she stepped out from behind the desk area, Deanne could see that she was tall and very pretty.

"I really need you girls to help out in the rec area. Some of the younger kids have a lot of pain, and it helps to be distracted with games and such. Some of the older kids just need someone their own age to talk with. You know what I mean?" Renee asked.

Deanne and Susan nodded. Deanne wished she could be down in the cafeteria, eating lunch with Kathy and Chris. She really didn't want to be on the oncology floor.

Renee led them into the rec room. She chatted all the way, giving them some details about the kids' schedules. "Larry has to be taken down to radiology at one o'clock. He's in room 404, bed C. Kyla needs a chemotherapy session at two o'clock. She's in room 416, bed B. And we need someone to help write letters for Karen, room 423, bed A. She's just had an operation on her eyes and the bandages are still in place."

Deanne listened. Every kid on the floor had some form of cancer. It was hard to believe and she felt nervous. When they reached the rec room, they went inside. It looked a lot like the rec rooms on the other floors. Three video games lined one wall. Patients stood and worked the controls. They seemed unaware of everyone else. Some were dressed in pajamas and robes, some in T-shirts and jeans. Most were between ten and fifteen years old.

Some were bald. Deanne knew that their hair loss had been caused by the treatments they were receiving. She swallowed hard and walked over to one tall boy bent over a video game.

She watched him move the controls and stare intensely at the video screen. "Hi," she said casually as soon as one of the video ghosts ate his electronic player.

He turned to her. She found herself looking into two beautiful blue eyes. They were set in a thin, pale face that was framed by a mass of thick brown hair. Somehow, he looked very familiar. "I'm Deanne," she said nervously.

"I'm Matt," he answered.

Suddenly, she knew where she had seen him before—in the lobby last spring! His whole family had been standing around his wheelchair! That had been several months before and he was still here! She felt her voice catch in her throat.

"You want to play this?" he asked.

"Against you?" she asked.

"Why not?" he shrugged his thin shoulders and pushed the button for playing doubles.

She watched him as he took his turn. Deanne felt a little shaken. He was a very good-looking guy. He was tall and she guessed he was about sixteen. It was hard to believe he'd been sick in the hospital for so long. She wanted to know more about him.

"Your turn," he said.

She took the controls and concentrated on the game.

Six

"You seem a million miles away," Susan said. Deanne glanced over at her friend and stopped twirling the straw in her soda.

"Oh, I don't know . . ." Deanne's voice trailed off.

"Those cancer kids really got to you, huh?" Susan asked.

Deanne dropped her eyes and shrugged her shoulders. "It's such a bummer, you know? Getting cancer when you're just a kid."

"Are you going to tell Mrs. Sanders you want off that floor?"

Deanne shook her head. "No. I don't think so. Even though I hate the way she 'volunteered' me, I think I'm going to hang around up there."

"That Matt is pretty cute, huh?" Susan asked, leaning over the table in the hospital cafeteria.

"He sure is," Deanne smiled. "I wonder what's wrong with him? You know, what kind of cancer does he have?"

"I don't know," Susan shrugged. "What's your plan for the rest of the day?"

Deanne looked at the clock. It was already four o'clock. "Dad usually leaves around six o'clock if he's not tied up. I think I'll just wait for him."

"I've got to catch the bus for home in twenty minutes," Susan said.

"Well," Deanne said as she stood up. "I think I'll go back up to oncology. Maybe I can talk to Matt again."

"Have fun," Susan urged. Then she added, "See ya tomorrow."

Deanne went up to the fourth floor and began looking for Matt. She found out at the front desk that he was assigned to room 438, bed A. But he wasn't there.

"He's down in chemotherapy," Renee Stewart offered. "I'm glad you came back on your own time, Deanne," she added. "He should be up shortly. The treatments often make him sick to his stomach. Sometimes it's nice to have somebody to talk to or play a game with . . . you know . . . to keep the patient's mind off the nausea. Can you wait for him?"

"Sure," Deanne nodded. "I'll be glad to hang around and wait. I'll get some board games out. Maybe he'd like to play something." Deanne paused. Then she cautiously asked, "He seems like such a nice guy. He is getting well, isn't he?"

"Matt Gleason?" Renee asked. "He's one of the nicest kids on the floor. Always has a smile and a friendly word. Do you know he sometimes sits for hours with some of the younger kids after their treatments when they're real sick, just so they won't be alone. Matt's a real giver; no matter what he's going through.

"As for him getting better, well, this is his third relapse since he was diagnosed with cancer five years ago. He's getting some new drugs, experimental medicines that have been useful against his type of malignancies. When he first checked in, we didn't think he'd make it through the summer. Now, we just don't know."

* * * * *

"You up to a friendly game of Scrabble?" Deanne came up to Matt as he sat in a wheelchair in the rec room.

He looked up at her. Her heart skipped and

her stomach fluttered. He looked so pale and ill. "You up to me beating you?" he asked weakly, trying to smile.

"Beat me?" Deanne cried in mock horror. "I'll have you know, I could beat you, blind-folded."

"You sure talk a good game," Matt whispered. He gripped the arms of the chair as a spasm swept over his body.

Deanne hurriedly sat down at the table and began spreading out the Scrabble board and letter holders. "Here," she said, offering him the bag of letter tiles. "Let's draw for first."

His hand was shaking, but he pulled out a letter. "It's a C," he said. "Can you beat that?"

She rummaged through the tiles and pulled out an X. "Hmm," she said. "I guess you're first." She paused, "But I'm still going to beat you."

"I want you to play your best," he warned. "I don't want you to feel sorry for me and let me win."

"Are you kidding?" Deanne protested. "I intend to trounce you. After all, I am a Vandervoort. I have a tradition to uphold. We Vandervoorts show no mercy."

"Good," Matt smiled weakly. "Because we Gleasons are fighters. I like being the under-dog." He leaned closer toward her. "It makes the pretty girls feel protective of me."

Deanne blushed. "I'm not a pretty girl," she said. "But I am a smart one. And I can't play my word until you play yours. So, get going."

They played for almost an hour. It was a good game. Deanne found him to be both competitive and smart. But she did win. "Not too shabby," Matt commented while she put away the board.

"Thanks," she smiled. "You weren't so bad yourself. You almost killed me with 'zither.' You got thirty-six points for that word alone."

"Are you going to give me a chance to get even?" Matt asked.

"Of course I will," Deanne smiled. "I work tomorrow. I'll be up here for the afternoon rec program. Maybe we could play then."

"Suits me," Matt said. "Maybe I'll read a dictionary before I go to bed tonight."

"Hey! Gleason! The supper trays are coming up. You eating?" A dark-haired nurse called from the doorway.

"I don't know . . .," his voice trailed off. "I'm kind of tired."

"You need to eat," the nurse chided.

"I have an idea," Deanne said quickly. "I need to eat supper, too." Her mind raced. If her dad wasn't ready for another half-hour, she could stay with Matt and encourage him to eat. Her mother would kill her for not eating at home, but it would be worth it if Matt would eat some of his food.

"Why don't I get a sandwich out of the machine and join you for dinner?" Deanne asked. The nurse caught on immediately.

"Great idea!" she added. "I'll even bring you a can of pop from the floor's private refrigerator."

"I could have my tray in here," Matt said thoughtfully. "I hate to eat alone."

"Good," Deanne said, jumping up. "It's settled. Let me go down to the sandwich machines and I'll be right back."

"I'll bring in your tray," the nurse told Matt.

Out in the hall, she turned to Deanne and said, "Thanks a lot. It's really important that he eats. After chemotherapy, it's kind of hard to think about food. It'll help to have you eat with him."

"Sure," Deanne said. She felt happy inside. She was glad to help Matt any way she could. But more than that, she realized that she liked him a lot. He was so nice.

"And he has cancer," she told herself quietly. But she didn't want to think about that right now. She just couldn't.

* * * * *

"But, Deanne, it's July Fourth weekend. The Cortlands have invited us to their place at the beach. We'll have such a good time," Mrs. Vandervoort said happily.

Deanne squirmed on the Victorian sofa and twisted her hands in her lap. She hated the formal living room, the Victorian sofa in particular. The fabric was scratchy and uncomfortable.

"I know, Mother," Deanne said. "But Dad can't go. He's got to stay at the hospital."

"All the more reason for you to come along," her mother stressed. "We'll go swimming and sailing and we'll play tennis. Besides, Judson will miss having someone his own age—"

"Mother, Judson doesn't even know I'm alive," Deanne said. "No. I just don't want to go. The hospital will be short of volunteers and regular staff, too. They need me."

"Deanne, you can't lock yourself away in that stuffy old hospital all summer! You're there morning, noon, and night already. This whole summer is slipping away and you haven't done anything that's fun for a girl your age. Now we both have the chance for a wonderful, few days vacation," said her mother.

"But, Mother," Deanne said as she stood up

and began pacing around the room. "Honest, I'm having a terrific summer! I have tons of friends at the hospital. You know my best friend, Susan. And all the nurses—and some of the patients—they're all my friends. I LIKE working at the hospital. I'd just be thinking about everybody the entire time I was away! What kind of company would I be at the Cortlands' anyway?" Deanne paused to catch her breath.

"There won't be anyone here, Deanne," Mrs. Vandervoort tried again. "I can't come running to pick you up. You'd have to be on your father's schedule. If he's stuck there at the hospital, then so are you."

"That's all right," Deanne said eagerly. "I know everybody. I can eat in the cafeteria, rest in Dad's office, even shower and change if I have to."

"Oh, honestly!" Mrs. Vandervoort said, throwing up her hands in defeat. "How can I convince you that your entire life is slipping by and you're not having any fun?" She paced across the plush carpets and stopped in front of the colonial fireplace.

"All right, Deanne," she said. "I'll discuss it with your father. If the two of you want to stay here over the July Fourth holiday, then fine. I'm going with the Cortlands and I plan to have a wonderful time!" Her mother turned and left the room.

Deanne plopped back down on the sofa. She felt tired, tired of always arguing with her mother, tired of being forced into a mold she hated. The hospital was all she really cared about, the hospital and Matt. He was a good friend. So was Susan.

But Susan wasn't "socially acceptable" and Matt had cancer. Her father understood when he wasn't too busy to listen. He knew what it was like to be involved with people.

She asked him about Matt one day, about the treatments and his future. "I'm not personally acquainted with the case," her father had said. "But, the first rule of nursing and doctoring is to never get personally involved with your patients. Sometimes it happens. But, the rule is: Don't do it."

Deep down in her heart, Deanne knew she had broken the first rule.

Seven

"You've lost weight," Matt said, more as a comment than a question. Deanne shrugged and leaned over to straighten up the blanket on the empty bed next to his.

"Yeah," she said, "a little." Secretly, she was excited that he'd noticed. She had lost ten pounds since the beginning of the summer. Her VolunTeen uniform pants were a size too large and she had to put on a belt to keep them from falling down.

"I'm sure looking forward to today," Matt said aloud. "You're going to like my parents and my sisters and brother."

Deanne smiled and nodded, but she was nervous. It had been Matt's idea to have a picnic on the hospital grounds for the Fourth of July. His doctors had thought it was a great idea. So, he told his mother and she packed up a picnic basket for them. Now they were on their way to the hospital to meet him. Matt's family had a summer home on a lake about fifty miles from All-Children's Hospital. They called often and came to visit once a week.

"Of course, you'll come, too," he had told Deanne when the picnic became official.

"Oh, no," she protested. "It's just for you and your family. I'd just be in the way."

"That's dumb!" Matt had said. "I want you to meet my family. Besides, you haven't got a better offer, have you?"

Deanne had blushed. "No, it's just that I don't want to, you know . . ."

"No, I don't know," Matt had said. "My mom makes the best fried chicken in the world. My sisters are dying to meet anyone who has beaten the Great Matt Gleason ten straight times in Scrabble. Come on, we'll have a good time. I promise."

Deanne had finally agreed. Now they were both waiting for his family to arrive and go to the small pond near the oak trees on the west side of the hospital. Deanne was both excited and nervous. She knew by the way Matt talked about them that his family was pretty special to him. She wanted them to like her.

"Matt!" A little blond-haired boy of four bounded across the room and took a flying leap into Matt's lap.

"Anthony!" Matt cried, rubbing his hands through the smiling child's white hair.

"Matt! Can I ride down with you in your wheelchair?" the boy cried, plopping into Matt's arms and touching the chair's big silver wheels.

"I think I could arrange that," Matt smiled. "What do you think, Deanne? Can you push us both?"

"Gee, I'm not sure," Deanne teased. "Maybe if Anthony promises to sing on the way down . . ."

"I will! I will!" Anthony shouted.

"And I've got news for you both," Matt said. "Just as soon as we're outside, I'm walking!"

Just then the rest of Matt's family came into the room. Once again, Deanne was struck by their strong resemblance. Everybody began talking at once.

Finally, Matt shouted, "Hey, wait a minute! Let's keep it down. There's someone here I want you to meet."

Deanne's eyes swept over the handsome group as Matt introduced her. His mom, Janet, was petite and pretty. She had short, dark hair and laugh lines around her eyes. Deanne liked her right away. His dad, Chuck, was a big man, with close-cropped hair and large, expressive hands. Deanne could see where all the kids got their beautiful eyes. His eyes were a deep, penetrating blue.

The oldest sister was thirteen-year-old Tina, then came ten-year-old Theresa. Next, she met Janette, who was nine, and Patricia, who was six. All of them had sandy-colored hair and bright blue eyes. Deanne couldn't remember seeing a more attractive, friendly, outgoing bunch of people.

"So glad to finally meet you, Deanne," Janet Gleason said warmly. "Matt's told us so much about you. We really appreciate all of the personal time you've spent with him."

Deanne blushed and smiled. "So, when's lunch?" Chuck Gleason asked. "I've been smelling that fried chicken all the way here from the lake house, and I'm starved!"

"Me, too!" Anthony chimed in. "Then, let's go!" Matt called, pushing his chair toward the door.

"Wait for me," Deanne said as she grasped the handles of the chair. Together, they all went down in the elevator and outside into the warm, sunlit summer day.

* * * * *

Matt was right. His mother did make the

best fried chicken in the world. Deanne loved the meal of fried chicken, potato salad, baked beans, watermelon, brownies, and plenty of ice-cold lemonade. Deanne thought she was going to burst. Everything tasted so good!

Two hours later, everyone had settled down to let the food digest. The four younger kids played ball. Matt and his dad went for a walk. Janet, Tina, and Deanne stretched out on the blanket under the shady oak trees.

Deanne couldn't remember feeling more content. She briefly thought of her mother at the Cortlands'. She started to feel guilty, but she pushed the thought aside. "We're all having a good time," she told herself. She was. And she knew her mom would be having a good time sailing. Her father was happy working at the hospital.

Janet Gleason spoke up, "Matt tells me you're part of the hospital's volunteer staff."

"Yes, I am," Deanne confirmed.

"Is it fun?" Tina asked.

"It's fabulous!" Deanne said. "It makes me feel busy and useful. I hate sitting around doing nothing all summer."

"I don't think I'd like to be around sick people all the time," Tina sighed. "What with Matt and all . . ." her voice trailed and she sniffed loudly.

Immediately, Deanne knew what she meant. "You don't think about how sick a patient is," Deanne told her. "You just think about how you can make him feel better."

"I can't stand to see Matt hurting," Tina continued.

"Matt's been sick for a very long time, Deanne," Janet said, patting Tina. "On again, off again. In the hospital, out of the hospital. He's well for months and then back for more radiation, chemicals, spinal taps . . ."

"Sometimes," Tina started, "I used to hate him." She paused. "Mom and Dad were with him all the time. My aunt and I were in charge of the others. It made me mad and I felt guilty, too. I was well and healthy. Matt wasn't."

"We have a wonderful minister," Janet explained. "He's helped us deal with Matt's illness, and our feelings about it. I don't know what we would have done if we hadn't had him."

"Don't you ever get angry with God?" Deanne asked. No one had ever talked to her as if she were an adult, as if she had feelings and thoughts about life.

"Why?" Tina asked. "It's not God's fault Matt's sick. Bad things happen to good people all the time. It's how the person faces up to the bad things that really matters. Matt's never hated God because he's sick. How can I?"

Deanne felt the impact of her words. She looked across the green grass at Matt and his father. They walked slowly. Their heads were close in conversation. Her heart went out to him. Her life was so perfect by comparison. If only she could tell her parents right then how she felt. If only . . .

* * * * *

The hospital halls were dim and quiet. Deanne could hear the hiss of oxygen coming from a room as she walked quietly down the corridor.

It had been such a full, exciting day: the picnic, the walks, and the games of Scrabble and Clue she'd played with the Gleason family. She'd had the best time of her life.

Matt's family was terrific. She liked them so much and they all liked her. But all the activity had really tired Matt, so he had gone back to his room and his family had left by seven o'clock.

Deanne checked to see when her father would be ready to leave, but a sudden emergency had put him in the operating room at seven-thirty. She went to his office and tried to watch TV for a while. Then she tried to sleep. But she couldn't do either.

So, she walked quietly down the halls, drawn like a magnet toward Matt's room. She slipped inside. She could see his resting form on the bed. Deanne slipped over to the side of his bed and looked down on him.

His arm was laying across his face, covering his forehead and his eyes. His mass of curly hair was laying against his pillow. She wanted to let him know how much she cared.

"Don't go." His voice startled her.

Deanne jumped back. "Oh, Matt. I'm so sorry. I-I didn't mean to wake you."

"I wasn't asleep," he said. "I hate to go to sleep anymore." He raised himself up on his elbow and peered at her through the darkness. She listened to his husky voice.

"Do you want me to get a nurse? She could give you something." Deanne suggested.

"No," Matt said. "You don't understand." He paused. Then he said, "When I was a little boy my mom taught me my first prayer. I'm sure you know it. It goes:

'Now I lay me down to sleep,
I pray the Lord my soul to keep;
If I should die before I wake,
I pray the Lord my soul to take.' "

"I know that one," Deanne nodded.

"One night it occurred to me that I could die in my sleep," Matt told her. "After that, I was so scared of going to sleep. I slept with a light on for months. Silly, huh?"

Deanne said nothing.

He continued. "And now—now I really might die in my sleep. I don't want to do that," he whispered. "If I die, I want it to be in the daylight. I want to meet the sun."

"Don't talk that way, Matt." Deanne reached out and took his hand. "You're not going to die."

He plopped back down onto the bed. "Could you stay with me for a while?" he asked. "Just for a while. Just until I get to sleep?"

"Of course, I can," Deanne said, squeezing his hand.

"Somehow, it's not so hard when someone's with me—when someone's holding on."

"I'll be right here," she told him. She pulled a chair over next to his bed, never letting go of his hand.

From down the hall, she could still hear the night sounds of the hospital.

Eight

"**D**ad, do people with cancer ever get well?" Deanne blurted out the question as her father sat reading in his wood-paneled study.

Dr. Vandervoort put down his medical journal and stared at his daughter. Deanne's face was troubled. She knew she must look worried. But she *had* to talk to someone about what she was feeling inside.

"Come sit down," her father said.

She went over to the brown leather sofa across from his desk and sat down. Its surface felt smooth and cool. She had always liked his study. It smelled of leather and old books. She felt warm and welcomed in the brown and navy blue-colored room.

"First of all," Dr. Vandervoort began, "cancer is not just one disease. It's a group of diseases. There are many kinds of cancers. A *cancer* is a group of mutant cells that begin to grow uncontrollably and crowd out normal cells. No one knows why it occurs in children."

Deanne nodded. She understood. But what she really wanted to know was if people were ever cured of cancer.

"And yes," her father continued, "people do get well. Sometimes they go into remission and it never comes back. Sometimes, we can operate then treat the patient with radiation and chemotherapy—and it's completely gone."

Deanne let out an audible sigh. Her father looked at her sharply. "But," he said in his most authoritative voice, "sometimes, despite all the treatments, all the surgery, all the skill and knowledge of an entire staff of medical experts, we can't save a cancer patient."

Deanne sagged in her seat. "Nevertheless," he said, "we *never* give up. We bombard the cancer with everything we've got. It's like war. The cancer's the invader, and we're there to throw it out."

"I wish you had a sure cure . . .," she began.

"So do I, Deanne. Every day I pray for a cure. But, while I'm waiting, I go on fighting."

The room grew silent. Deanne could hear the ticking of the clock on his bookshelves. "Something tells me you have a particular cancer case in mind," Dr. Vandervoort said into the silence.

She dropped her eyes. "Oh, not really. It's just that I've been doing a lot of work on the oncology floor, and I feel so sorry for some of the kids."

"Don't let pity cloud your ability to serve," he told her.

"I don't understand."

"You're there to do a job, to help any way you can. Listen to your patients' needs and help them. Don't feel sorry for them. You're not doing them any favors, believe me."

Deanne wasn't quite sure what her father meant, but she was glad she talked to him. At least she now had some hope for Matt, hope that he really might get well.

* * * * *

"Deanne! Come quick! Pam Miller's locked herself in her bathroom and Mrs. Stewart can't get her to come out!" Susan's excited voice preceded her into the hospital room where Deanne was making up a bed.

"Oh, no!" Deanne cried and raced down the hall behind her friend. Together they burst into room 409, Pam's room.

"Pam! Pam Miller! You open this door right now!" Nurse Stewart said as she pounded on the hard door surface.

"What's going on?" Deanne asked.

"Pam woke up this morning and huge wads of her hair were laying on her pillow."

"Oh, no," Deanne said.

"Yes, it's the chemotherapy. She knew it might happen. But I guess it's hard when you're only fifteen and your hair is your crowning glory. Pam!" she called through the door again, "Please open up!"

"No!" Pam shouted back. "Go away! I'm never coming out! I swear!"

"Can I try?" Deanne asked nervously. "I've worked with her a lot. We've kind of gotten to be friends."

"Sure," Mrs. Stewart said. Then she added, "Quick, Susan, go down to maintenance and get someone to bring some tools. We may have to take the door off the hinges."

Deanne went over to the door and called, "Pam? Pam? It's me, Deanne. What's going on?"

"Go away!" Pam shouted back. "I'm never coming out! I tell you, NEVER!"

"Well, why not?" Deanne asked, trying hard to think of a way to get Pam to open the door.

"Because I'm BALD!" Pam wailed. "I—I look hideous!"

"But, Pam, you can't stay in there. What about the stuff we planned to do this afternoon?"

"I can't do anything! Paul is supposed to come today. I can't let him see me like this!" Pam started to cry.

Paul! Of course! Deanne thought. Paul was her boyfriend.

"Oh, Pam, Paul won't care. I know he won't. Why you, Paul, Matt, and I have even talked about it. You know he likes you just the way you are."

"That's easy for you to say," Pam sobbed. "He's never seen me bald. Besides, you have lots of beautiful blond hair!"

Deanne gave a start. She never once thought of her hair as beautiful. It was so limp and baby fine. But it must seem glorious to someone who is going bald. "You know it will grow back," Deanne tried again. "Matt's fell out and it all grew back, even nicer than before, he says. Now, please unlock the door."

"Go away!" Pam shouted.

Deanne searched her thoughts for an idea. Pam was a nice girl, very outgoing and with a good sense of humor. Deanne remembered that she often talked about becoming an actress. Pam had been in many school plays and loved the theater.

"You know," Deanne began. "If you never come out, I won't be able to use you in the special play

75

Mrs. Coffman asked me to help her with."

There was silence. "It's a neat play," Deanne continued. She made up what she was going to say quickly. "It's going to be about life here on the oncology floor told from the patient's point of view. We were talking about asking you to be the star."

"Really?" Pam asked.

"Sure," Deanne said, crossing her fingers. "You know what we're going to call it?"

"What?" Pam asked.

"Hairless," Deanne said in her most deadpan voice.

Suddenly, Deanne heard a little snicker come from beyond the door. "W-What?" Pam asked. Deanne could tell Pam was trying not to laugh.

"Hairless," she repeated. "In fact, the only reason we were hesitant about using you is because you had all your hair . . .," she paused. Then she heard a click. The door slowly swung open and Pam stood there looking out at her.

"In a few weeks, I'll look like Telly Savalas," Pam muttered.

Her long hair hung in clumps. Deanne could see several bald spots on her head. "Then I guess you'll be just right for the part," Deanne smiled broadly.

Pam gave a half laugh. "You could say that."

"Come on, Pam," Mrs. Stewart said, taking her hand. "Let's sit down and talk about it."

She led the girl across the room to a chair. "I'm sorry," Pam said.

"It's all right," Mrs. Stewart told her. "It's tough, I know. But you're not alone. Many, many kids lose their hair with the treatments. It's a small price to pay if you get well, isn't it?"

Pam nodded. "It's *only* hair," she said. "I can get a wig."

"Or wear a scarf," Deanne added. "You're still YOU."

"*Hairless,* huh?" Pam said with a half-smile.

"Thanks," Mrs. Stewart said to Deanne. "You can go on now."

"Listen," Deanne said as she neared the doorway. "Matt and I will still be waiting for you and Paul in the rec room this afternoon. Want to play some Scrabble?"

"Sure," Pam smiled. "It'll keep my mind off my problems."

Deanne hurried off down the hall to go find Matt and tell him about her adventure.

* * * * *

Deanne became a minor celebrity among

the nurses and volunteer staff. She kept her cool and talked a patient out of a potentially dangerous situation.

Everyone seemed to know her and admired her for her fast thinking. "I said the first thing I thought of," she told Susan. "I remembered that she liked plays and stuff so I said the part about her starring in a made-for-the-hospital play. I'm just glad she thought it was funny and came out."

A few days later, while she was on her way to take Matt down for a radiation treatment, she heard her name called from an open doorway.

"Miss Vandervoort." Deanne froze in her tracks. The voice was that of Mrs. Sanders.

"I would like a word with you, Miss Vandervoort," the voice called out. Slowly, Deanne turned to face the tall, starched form of Lillie Sanders.

"Y-Yes, Mrs. Sanders," she said.

"I've heard about your recent action with the young patient in oncology." Deanne felt her heart pounding.

Mrs. Sanders's face broke into a smile. "Good work!"

Deanne sighed with relief. "Thank you, Mrs. Sanders," she said.

"In fact, I was impressed with your suggestion. I've told the Child-Life Specialist, Mrs. Coffman, that she should get with you and the two of you should write such a play."

"What?" Deanne gasped.

"It's a good idea," Mrs. Sanders continued. "These patients need a way to express their feelings about the doctors, the hospital, the treatments—everything that's happening to them. A play is a great way to do it. We have video cameras, TV sets, plenty of kids to play the different roles. Yes, I think a play we could record on videocassette for incoming patients about cancer would be a wonderful idea.

"I want you to get with Mrs. Coffman today. You can start planning it. I want you to help write it and pick out kids for the different roles. And why not call it *Hairless?* It's the truth, isn't it?"

Deanne stood staring at her with her mouth open. "Well, run along," Mrs. Sanders said crisply. "Get your work done, then go see Mrs. Coffman. You two have a lot of work to do."

Nine

"Pam, I want you to act like nothing's strange about a roomful of doctors playing video games while the patient lies on the operating table waiting for surgery," Mrs. Coffman said. She stood in the room directing the actors for the portable TV cameras.

Deanne giggled and glanced down at the clipboard. They already shot seven scenes and the production was going smoothly. She had to admit that she had been scared to death of the project when Mrs. Sanders had told her to do it. But, after discussing it with Clare Coffman, she became excited about doing it.

The play had been fun, planning it, writing it, and getting the kids together. Pam had been chosen to be the Narrator. She would guide the viewer through an imaginary day in the life of an oncology patient.

The script was outrageous. There was a lot

of fun made of the staff, the hospital, the treatments, and each other. Once Deanne had started talking about it to the kids on the oncology floor, suggestions about how to make it funny flowed like water.

Pam decided to play the part of the Narrator without wearing either a scarf or a wig. Her head was covered with a brown fuzz and she seemed proud to show it off.

"Very good!" Clare shouted as the kids played the roles of the doctors and ignored the guy playing the patient on the operating table. Their scrub clothes hung down to the floor and the patient lay wrapped in a sheet. He pleaded for the doctors to hurry up. "I tell you, I can't wait all day," the patient yelled according to his script. "I must get back to my room! It's lunch time!"

"Cut!" Clare called. "Excellent! Deanne, where do we go from here?"

Deanne checked off the scene they just finished and said, "Let's see. We need to go to a room so the Dietician can serve lunch."

"Okay," said Clare. "Who's playing the Dietician?"

Matt stepped forward. "I am," he said.

The troupe of actors, cameramen, staff, and assistants went upstairs into a room already brightly lit for the new scene.

"In bed, patient," Clare directed.

The kid actors took their places. "Camera and . . . action," Clare announced.

"Here we have the typical patient resting comfortably and waiting for her meal to arrive," Pam said from her memorized script. The bed was aimed at a cockeyed angle so that the patient looked folded up in the bed.

Matt, as the Dietician, came into the room carrying a large tray heaped with thick cardboard cutouts of different food items.

"I have a wonderful meal for you!" he announced. He put the tray down on the patient's bedstand.

"It looks so stiff and unappetizing," the patient said.

"You vill eat this or you vill be shot!" Matt shouted in a thick German accent.

Deanne kept stifling her laughter. She was having a great time and so was everybody else.

On cue, Susan rushed into the room carrying a three-foot-long foam rubber syringe. She yelled, "Shot! Shot! Did someone say shot?"

"Cut!" Clare called out. "Terrific, kids!" That was just terrific."

Deanne checked that scene off on her clipboard. "Now we need the VolunTeens giving the patient a sponge bath," Deanne said.

Two younger kids, dressed in the familiar VolunTeen outfit, came forward carrying a basin of water, a rubber duck, and a blow dryer.

Pam began her narration. "One of the best parts of a patient's day is when the friendly, helpful VolunTeen staff arrives to give the patient a nice, quiet sponge bath in bed."

Immediately, the two VolunTeens began bickering over who was carrying the bowl. "I'll do it!" the first VolunTeen shouted.

"No, you won't! I'll do it!" the second VolunTeen shouted back. They both kept tugging at the bowl they carried between them.

The bowl was dumped right on the patient's lap. "Now look what you've done!" the patient shouted.

"Oops!" said the first VolunTeen.

"So start sponging!" cried the second VolunTeen. Together, the two girls began rubbing the struggling patient all over with the sponge. Then, they turned on the blow dryer and aimed that at the patient.

"Cut!" Clare called out. "Outstanding!" she cried. "Oh, you all are really doing a terrific job. Just wait until we sit down and see the finished tape! You will be so proud."

The day seemed to fly by. Deanne ran around to help set up scenes. She reminded the actors of forgotten lines. She got cans of pop and snacks for everyone working on the project. By five o'clock the production was complete.

"It's a wrap!" Clare called. "*Hairless* is officially 'in the can!'"

The group clapped, cheered, and whistled. "Now, I'll edit it. I think we'll be ready to officially view it in a couple days."

"We need to have a premier party," Pam said.

"Good idea!" Clare agreed. "Who should we invite?"

Everybody started talking at once. "Hold it! Hold it!" Clare laughed. "Deanne, help plan this thing!"

Deanne called out, "I need a committee. You, you, you, and you," she said, pointing to various faces. "Tomorrow, at two o'clock in the rec room, we'll plan the party."

"The gala opening of *Hairless!*" someone shouted. Another cheer went up. Deanne beamed. She had never had more fun.

* * * * *

"Are you okay?" Deanne came quietly into Matt's room and walked over to his bed.

"Sure," Matt whispered. But Deanne could

tell he was in pain.

"I missed you after we finished taping this afternoon." Deanne said.

"I was feeling a little tired."

"Matt," she reached out for his hand. "My father's waiting down in the lobby for me. I've got to go home. But I'll be back first thing in the morning. Can I call you later tonight?"

He squeezed her hand weakly. "It's all right," he said painfully. "I'll be okay until tomorrow." Beads of sweat stood out on his forehead.

Deanne felt a lump rise in her throat. She felt so helpless! She wanted him to stop hurting. "Did you have a good time today?" she asked.

"Sure," he whispered. "You wrote a great script. I can't wait to see it all put together."

Deanne ached inside for him. She could think of nothing else to say. "I-I have to go," she said. "I'll see you tomorrow."

"If I should die before I wake," he said with a half-laugh.

"Oh, Matt, don't say that!" Deanne pleaded. She squeezed his hand and left the room.

It had been an interesting day. They taped a twenty minute video play about cancer. They made fun of all the things that kids with cancer had to endure. Everyone had fun doing it, too. They had laughed and joked about a very serious topic. Deanne hurried down to meet her father.

* * * * *

The auditorium was crowded. Doctors, nurses, patients, parents, and hospital staff were all waiting to see the production of *Hairless*. Deanne squirmed in her seat. She was nervous. So many people had shown up! Even her own parents were there.

Mrs. Vandervoort, smiling and waving at all the people she knew, sat next to Deanne in the auditorium. Deanne silently wished it would start. The waiting was the hardest part.

Matt and his family sat two rows in front of them. Deanne had talked to all his sisters and his brother when they first arrived. She also introduced the Gleasons to her parents.

"You must be very proud of Deanne," Janet Gleason smiled. "Matt tells me she helped write and produce this entire show. And I heard she thought of the idea in the first place."

Deanne blushed. Mrs. Vandervoort looked at her with surprise.

"Why, no," her mother said, "Deanne only

said she helped work on the story."

"Well, according to Matt, she was the driving force behind the project." Janet paused. Then she added, "You know, I'm glad to finally meet you. Deanne has been such a good influence on Matt. She's been a real friend to him and so helpful. With the kids and all, I can't get to the hospital as much as I want. But Deanne's been here every day. I just wanted you to know what a fine girl my husband and I think you've raised."

"Why, thank you," Mrs. Vandervoort said. She sounded impressed. Deanne had only blushed, waved at Matt, and gone back to her seat. Now, sitting and waiting for the production to start was making her nervous.

Suddenly the lights dimmed and the big-screen TV lit up. The show was on.

Deanne watched the show. She thought it was funny. But the reaction of the audience surprised her most of all. They loved it! They laughed and clapped and stomped during the different scenes. Everybody seemed to recognize themselves and think it was funny. Deanne was thrilled.

When it was over and the lights came back up, the audience actually cheered. Clare Coffman walked to the front of the auditorium. "Let's give a big hand to the real stars of this production!" she cried. "All you kids, my actors and actresses, my assistants, my camera people, all of you, please stand up and be recognized!"

Deanne got to her feet. Pam stood up. So did Matt, Susan, Carl, Todd, Mary, and all the helpers on the project. The audience clapped and clapped. They shouted, "Bravo!" They made all the participants feel wonderful!

Afterward, during refreshments, many came over to Deanne and told her, "Great job." "Nice work." "Watch out, Hollywood." Deanne beamed. She felt so proud and so happy. She did a good job and had a lot of fun doing it.

Mrs. Sanders came over and told both Dr. Vandervoort and Mrs. Vandervoort. "Your daughter is a fine nurse. She really cares about her patients. It showed tonight in that play."

Dr. Vandervoort smiled warmly at Deanne and told her, "I'm proud of you, honey. You helped them do a fine job."

Only her mother seemed a little withdrawn. Mrs. Vandervoort congratulated Deanne, but she also seemed preoccupied.

"Did you like the play?" Deanne asked

when they were riding home.

"Oh, yes," her mother said. "Very much." They rode a while in silence. Then her mother said, "I had no idea how involved you were with the hospital. I mean, I know you spend a lot of time there, but I didn't realize how much everyone thinks of you." Then she added softly, "You're not a little girl anymore."

They drove on into the night.

Ten

"**A**re you looking forward to going back to school?" Matt asked Deanne one afternoon.

"Not particularly," Deanne replied. She shifted in her chair and smiled at him.

Matt was sitting in a semi-reclining position in a special chair in the Chemotherapy Department. A long plastic tube reached from his arm to a bag of fluids hung on a rack next to his chair.

"It's not much longer now before school starts," he said.

"Right after Labor Day," she agreed. "But I'd rather stay here at the hospital than go back to a boring old classroom."

"What!" Matt asked in mock horror. "And become the *only* Vandervoort not to get a diploma?"

Deanne chuckled. "You're silly," she said.

Then she asked, "What will you do?"

"Get tutoring. I wish I could go back to school."

Deanne understood what he meant. "You've been here a long time," she said.

"Too long," he told her. "The worst part is I don't think I'm getting any better."

"Of course you are," Deanne protested.

A half-smile crossed his thin, handsome face. "I sure don't feel like I'm getting any better." They both were silent. Finally, Matt spoke. "You know," he said, "what I'd really like to do before this summer's over is go up to Loch de Nor."

"Your parents' place at the lake?" Deanne asked. She remembered hearing his whole family talk about their lake home.

"Deanne," Matt began, his blue eyes shining, "it's so beautiful up there. Ever since I was a little kid, we've been going to North Lake, that's what Loch de Nor means, you know. Even before I got sick we went there. I used to take the canoe and paddle along the shoreline for hours, just exploring. I found one place—that's just incredible. You'd have to see it to believe it. It's fantastic! I wish I could show you Loch de Nor . . .," his voice trailed off. Matt took a deep breath. Deanne could tell he wasn't feeling well.

"I'd love to see it!" Deanne cried. She didn't want him to lose his enthusiasm. "What's your house like there?"

"It's just a house. Anthony and I share a room. Tina, Theresa, Janette, and Patricia share rooms, too. Old Anthony's spoiled, he's had the room all to himself this summer."

"Maybe you'd better check yourself out and go re-stake your claim," Deanne teased.

"I would in a minute, if my doctors would let me." He paused. "We do lots of stuff as a family," he continued. "We play Hearts and Monopoly and every outdoors game you can think of."

Deanne felt a twinge of jealously. She couldn't imagine a big family playing and having fun together like Matt said. Her childhood had been so different. "I like your family," she said. "Tina's very pretty."

"Don't I know it. Last summer this guy who lives over on the other side of the lake used to come all the way around every day at noon just to talk with Tina when she walked out to the mailbox."

Deanne giggled. "I'd be flattered," she said.

"Are you trying to tell me that no one would walk all the way around the lake to see you?" he teased.

Deanne blushed. "Don't be silly! Besides, who's got time for that?"

"For love?" he asked.

"Stop it!" Deanne protested.

"You're blushing! Did I hit a nerve? Ah, so there is someone special!" he said triumphantly.

"No one you know," Deanne said in a huff.

"Will you see him when school starts?"

"He doesn't go to my school."

"Someone here at the hospital?"

She glared at him. Her face was red. "I told you there's no one special. Now knock it off!"

"Hey! Hey! What's all the racket?" asked one of the nurses as she poked her head in the room.

Matt and Deanne looked at her. "Patients on chemotherapy are supposed to be kept quiet," she told Deanne. "You know that."

Deanne swallowed hard.

"It was my fault," Matt said. "I'll keep calm. I promise."

The nurse gave them a stern look, then left.

"Sorry," he said.

Deanne shrugged. "Me, too."

"Friends?" Matt asked.

"Forever," she smiled back.

"Forever," he whispered.

* * * * *

"Ugh! I hate the thought of going back to school." Susan sipped her pop and made a face at Deanne.

"I know," Deanne sighed. "Me, too."

"I don't know why my parents insist on keeping me in that fancy prep school anyway," Susan grumbled. "Mother works, Dad works . . . just to send me to some silly rich kids' school. I'd much rather go to a public school."

"You never told me that!" Deanne said, surprised.

Susan glanced down. "I know," she said. "I shouldn't say it now. You can't help it if you're rich. You know, when the summer started and you started to work here at the hospital, I couldn't believe it."

"What do you mean?" Deanne asked.

"Well, you have so much. Why would you want to do volunteer work? It didn't make any sense."

"I would have never done it if you hadn't encouraged me," Deanne said sincerely.

Susan smiled. "I'm glad you did. Otherwise, we'd never have become friends." She took a big sip of pop through her straw. "I'll bet you've logged more hours than any VolunTeen in the program."

"It's been fun. I've never thought of it as work."

"Still, when Pat Jacobson gives out the service awards next month, I'll bet you get the most."

"I wish we didn't have to go back to school," Deanne said, changing the subject. "I'll miss everyone."

"Especially Matt," Susan finished.

"Especially Matt," Deanne agreed. "But I am going to work on Saturdays and after school."

"Yeah. Me, too. Next summer, I'll be old enough to get a paying job. So, this may be my last fling with volunteer work," Susan added.

Deanne felt sorry for Susan. She was glad she could afford to be a VolunTeen, glad that she could work at the hospital for as long as she wanted. All in all, Deanne realized that she had a lot to be thankful for.

* * * * *

Mrs. Vandervoort paced around the living room. Dr. Vandervoort stood leaning against the fireplace. Deanne watched the whole scene, her heart beating.

Matt's family had asked her to spend the entire Labor Day weekend with them at Loch de Nor! She was so excited, she could hardly sit still. The whole weekend! Best of all, Matt's doctors had given him a seventy-two hour pass from the hospital so that he could go, too.

"I don't know," her mother said, shaking her head.

"Mr. Gleason came to me personally," Dr. Vandervoort told her. "He said that Matt had asked especially for Deanne to come stay with his sisters. It means a lot to the boy."

"But the whole weekend," Mrs. Vandervoort protested. "Hans, we don't even know these people."

"I know plenty," he assured his wife. "They're a fine family with a very sick son who wants to go home for a few days. He wants our daughter to come, too. It's no different than letting her go spend the weekend with your sister, Christine."

"But, Christine's family," Mrs. Vandervoort said.

"The Gleasons are family to me," Deanne said quickly. "I'll be staying with Matt's sister, Tina, the whole time. Oh, please let me go! Mother, I want to go! I'm almost fifteen. I know how to act. I won't embarrass the Vandervoort name, you know."

"That's not the point, Deanne," her mother began. "It's—it's just not proper."

"Why not? You wanted to take me to spend a whole weekend with Judson Cortland over July Fourth."

"That was different . . ."

"Hold it!" Dr. Vandervoort said in his deep authoritative voice. "You're my family, and I will decide."

Both Mrs. Vandervoort and Deanne looked at him. "Sylvia, I see no reason why Deanne can't go. She's a mature, smart girl. The Gleasons are caring people and their son is very sick. They'll take good care of both of them. I want her to go."

Mrs. Vandervoort started to say something. But she changed her mind when he turned his determined face toward her. Deanne wanted to jump up and hug him.

"Very well," Mrs. Vandervoort said finally. "I'll speak to Mrs. Gleason and make the arrangements. Maybe you're right, Hans. Deanne's grown up a lot this summer. Maybe this is the perfect thing for her to do."

Eleven

Deanne had never seen any place more beautiful than Loch de Nor. The lake was large and deep navy blue in color. Its shoreline was lined with tall pines on its west bank and grass on its east bank. Homes and cottages dotted various clearings all around it.

The long shadows of evening were stretching across the shores of the lake when the Gleason family car pulled into the driveway. The ride from town had taken ninety minutes. It had tired Matt. As the car arrived, the Gleason kids, five of them, tumbled out the front door of the cabin.

"Matt! Matt!" Anthony shouted, hanging on the car window.

"Hi, guy," Matt smiled, tussling his brother's hair.

His father opened the car door for Deanne and Matt. "Wait a minute, Tiger," Chuck laughed. "Don't knock your brother over before he has a chance to get out of the car."

Everyone began talking at once. They were all so glad to have Matt home, even if it was only for three days. Janet hugged Deanne warmly and told Tina to get her suitcase.

"We're having 'sketti for supper!" Anthony shouted.

"'Sketti?" Matt laughed. "You mean, spaghetti?"

"Yeah! And cake, too! I helped."

"How?" Deanne asked.

"I licked the bowl!" Anthony said patiently.

Everyone laughed then filed inside. The family room was large and spacious. It led into a big country kitchen filled with the delicious aromas of hot garlic bread and tomato sauce.

"Come put your things in my room," Tina urged, leading Deanne down a hallway and into a green and white decorated bedroom. "I'm so glad you're here!"

"Me, too!" Deanne said. She tossed her things onto one of the twin beds and looked around. The room was neat, colorful, and clean. "Where's your sister staying?"

"Oh, Mom put up a cot in Patricia and Janette's room, just for this weekend, so we can have more space. It'll give us a chance to visit away from my little sisters' prying ears."

Deanne laughed and gave Tina a hug. "Thanks, I really like it here."

The family sat down to a huge dinner. Everyone seemed to talk and laugh at once. Deanne remembered her own family's quiet, simple meals. This was so much fun!

Anthony wanted to sit on Matt's lap. He kept patting his brother, as if he were making sure he was really there. Janette talked on and on about how fast she could go down the hill on her bike. Janet kept smiling at Matt.

Across the fireplace mantle they had strung a long homemade sign. It read: "Welcome Home, Matt." The room was homey and inviting. Deanne was grateful to be there.

After dinner, Mr. Gleason said, "I believe I could go for a game of hearts. Anyone else?"

Everyone shouted "Yes!" In minutes, the table was cleared, the dishwasher loaded, and everyone was seated back around the big oak table. A deck of cards was dealt. Deanne found it to be the most exciting game of hearts she'd ever played! She laughed so hard her sides hurt when Mr. Gleason got stuck with the queen of hearts.

"You lose! You lose!" Anthony shouted.

"Never!" Mr. Gleason said. "I can't lose! I'm the boss around here!"

They played a second game and a third. It

was ten o'clock before they knew it. Deanne was tired, but she felt content as she went off to bed.

Matt looked pale, but he seemed happy. Deanne was about to go into Tina's room when Matt caught her arm. "You an early riser?" he whispered.

"Well . . . uh . . . sure," she said.

"Good. Let's have an early breakfast, then I want to take you someplace special," he whispered.

"Where?" she probed.

"You'll see," he said, tapping her lightly on the nose. "It's a secret. But wear your walking shoes."

* * * * *

The canoe sliced through the water like a knife. Deanne watched as Matt dipped the oar into the smooth lake water to propel the canoe forward. The rising morning sun peeked over the tops of the pine trees. The smells of woods, water, and wild grass filled the air. The day promised to be hot.

Deanne didn't know where Matt was taking her. But she didn't care. It was a beautiful, golden summer morning. And they were together, skimming the shoreline of the lake. She was filled with anticipation.

"It's not much further," Matt said over his shoulder.

Deanne didn't care. She was content to sit back and glide along in the canoe. She hardly slept all night, anyway. She had been so excited about being with the Gleasons. She hated to waste her time sleeping.

It had been easy to get up at six in the morning. She met Matt in the kitchen and fixed them both scrambled eggs and toast. They'd been very quiet. They didn't want to wake up anyone else. Matt had left his mom a note. It said: "Took Deanne on a little canoe trip. We'll be home for lunch. Don't worry. Love, Matt."

"Look!" Matt shouted. He pointed to a flock of ducks. Deanne watched as they arched gracefully over the face of the lake water and soared up into the bright morning sky.

"They're beautiful!" Deanne cried.

"We're almost there," Matt said.

"Where?" she asked.

"You'll see . . ."

The canoe slowed. Matt backwashed the paddle. Then he aimed the canoe into the bank between two clumps of trees. The canoe hit the land with a gentle thump.

"Come on," Matt urged, stepping out of the boat and pulling Deanne by the hand. "We've got to walk a little ways."

The underbrush was thick, but Deanne tagged along after Matt. In a few minutes she was breathing hard and starting to perspire. But she pushed through the bushes behind him.

Matt stopped suddenly. "Wait," he said, gasping for breath.

"Are you all right?" she asked, alarmed.

"Sure," he gasped. "Just need to catch my breath. It's okay. Really. Besides . . . we're here."

"We're where?" asked Deanne hesitantly.

"At my special place. Close your eyes and give me your hand."

She obeyed. "Now don't peek," he said. "Follow me."

Deanne held on tightly as he led her along. Finally, he said, "Open up."

Deanne did. They were standing in a clearing in the forest. A carpet of pine needles covered the ground like a soft blanket. Tall, age-old firs and pines reached high overhead. They were so dense and thick that the sky was completely hidden. Long shafts of thick yellow sunlight hung in the air like taut ribbons. The air was cool.

It was so peaceful and beautiful that Deanne could hardly speak. Finally she said, "Oh, Matt! It's . . . it's . . . magnificent!"

"I know," he whispered. "I discovered it one

summer years ago. It's like a cathedral, isn't it?"

Deanne walked around the small clearing, looking up at the dark, green trees. She touched the trunks. She cupped her hands under a stream of sunlight and let it collect in a golden pool.

"Come here," he said as he sat down on an old log.

Deanne sat next to him and he took her hand. Her heart pounded, and her knees felt weak.

"I've never shown this place to anyone," he told her. "Never." He put his arm around her shoulders. She rested her head on his chest.

"Thank you for bringing me," she whispered. "Somehow, it didn't seem right that no one else should see it. Especially since I don't think I'll ever see it again."

She let out a cry and pushed away from him. "Matt! No . . ."

"It's all right, Deanne. I'm not afraid," he said, pulling her close.

"Please don't," she begged, tears brimming in her eyes.

"You've been a good friend to me," he said. "You've made these last few months the best. Thanks."

His chin rested on the top of her head. She lay her head back onto his chest. She could hear the beating of his heart.

"I used to wonder," he continued softly. "I still wonder . . . what it would be like to grow old . . . ."

Tears escaped her eyes and trickled down her cheeks. "Hey," he smiled, cupping her face in one of his hands. "Don't cry. It's all right. Really. I just wanted you to know that I'm not scared. I wanted to bring you here and show you this place."

His arms tightened around her again. They stood like that for a long time, letting time and summer wash over them. His mouth brushed her ear. "We've got to get back," he whispered.

She looked up at him. He looked pale. "Why don't I paddle home?" she offered. Then she added more lightly, "That is, if you trust me not to capsize the boat."

"I trust you," his smile looked pained. Deanne took his hand and headed back into the undergrowth, toward the canoe. She sniffed loudly and took a deep breath. Somehow she knew that she had to be the strong one now.

Matt lay down in the canoe and Deanne began to paddle back toward his house. It was longer to follow the shoreline, but she felt safer going that way. By the time she paddled back, her arms and shoulders ached. But she kept up a constant stream of chatter. It kept Matt's mind off how bad he felt

Mr. Gleason rushed into the water and grabbed the front of the canoe as it glided up. "He doesn't feel well," Deanne called out.

"I-I'm okay." "Matt whispered weakly.

"All right, son," his father said, grabbing him under his arm and hoisting him up. "Lie down inside for a while. You'll be all right." He helped Matt into the house.

Later, Janet fixed lunch, but no one had much of an appetite. They tried to play some basketball in the afternoon, but everyone kept thinking about Matt. He still didn't feel better.

During supper, there was hardly any conversation. Afterward, they tried to play hearts. The game seemed slow and boring. No one could concentrate. Janet kept checking on Matt all evening. About nine o'clock she sat down at the table. Her face looked very worried.

"Chuck," she said, leaning over toward her husband, "Matt wants to go back to the hospital. I think we should leave right now."

Twelve

The rest of the evening became a blur in Deanne's mind. They laid Matt in the backseat of the car. Janet sat, holding his head in her lap. "Deanne," Mr. Gleason said, "you'd better come back with us. You can call your folks from the hospital."

Then he turned to Tina and put his arm around her. "Honey," he began intensely, "we're leaving you in charge. Mom's called Mrs. Colwell. She's on stand-by, if you need her. We'll call you all just as soon as we get Matt to All-Children's."

"Dad," Tina began, her eyes filling with tears. "Matt will be all right, won't he?"

"Of course, he will!" Mr. Gleason said with a smile. "He's just overtired. They'll fix him up at the hospital. Now don't worry. And get the kids in bed."

Deanne sat tensely in the moving car. She

watched the darkness speed by. She could hear Matt's shallow breathing from the backseat. She was scared.

When they got to All-Children's, the orderlies whisked Matt upstairs to his room for tests. Deanne and the Gleasons nervously paced the hallway. It seemed like a nightmare to Deanne.

Hours before, she had been holding onto Matt in a sun-dappled forest clearing. Now, they were back at the hospital. And Matt was very sick. She swallowed the lump in her throat.

"Deanne, honey," Janet Gleason said softly. "Maybe you'd better call your parents and let them know where you are."

Deanne nodded and glanced at the clock on the wall. It was eleven-thirty. She didn't want to call. She didn't want them to make her come home. Her father answered the phone. Quickly, Deanne told him about Matt.

"I'll be right there," Dr. Vandervoort said. Deanne felt better. Her father would know what to do. All of Matt's doctors would listen to him. Together they'd make Matt well again.

* * * * *

All night long, doctors, lab technicians and nurses went in and out of Matt's room. Deanne could see the doctors conferring with each other through the door, whenever it opened. Dr. Vandervoort arrived and joined the quiet talks.

About four o'clock that morning Dr. Vandervoort and the two main physicians on Matt's case came over to the Gleasons. Deanne stood next to them.

"He's stabilized," Dr. Gallagher told them.

"Thank God," Janet said.

"That's good, isn't it, Daddy?" Deanne asked.

Dr. Vandervoort took her by her shoulders and stared at her with his piercing blue eyes. He said, "Yes, Matt's holding on. But, Deanne, he is very, very sick."

Her heart pounded. "Will he . . . could he . . .?" she couldn't say the word.

"We don't know. But he's resting now, and so should you."

"Oh, Dad!" she cried. "Please don't make me go home. Please let me stay till Matt's awake."

He looked hard at her. "I will," he said. "But go lie down in my office for a while. Someone will come and get you if there's a change."

Deanne nodded numbly. She was very tired. She knew she'd feel better if she got some sleep. She went to her father's office.

* * * * *

All the next morning there was no change in Matt's condition. Deanne had breakfast with the Gleasons in the hospital cafeteria. No one was very hungry. Since it was the Sunday before Labor Day, there wasn't much activity in the hospital. Only a bare minimum staff was working.

There were hardly any of the familiar faces Deanne was used to seeing. She wished Mrs. Stewart was there, and Susan, too. Vaguely, she remembered Susan telling her that the Pyle family was going to the beach over the long weekend.

Deanne felt all alone. She sat in the fourth floor rec room. She looked over the familiar games, tables, and chairs. She remembered all the fun and good times she and Matt had there. Deanne lifted up the Scrabble game and carefully laid it out. She set it up, as if they were going to play. She ran her fingers over the smooth letter tiles.

"Deanne." She looked up at the sound of her name. It was her mother. Mrs.

Vandervoort stood in the doorway. Her hair was perfectly groomed. She wore a white cotton skirt and a red silk blouse. *All crisp and clean and fresh,* Deanne thought.

"Hello, Mother," Deanne sighed.

"I wanted to check on you. You look so tired."

Deanne leaped up. "I'm not going home!" she cried defensively. "I'm going to stay here until Matt gets well!"

Mrs. Vandervoort bit her lower lip. "I didn't come to make you go home," she said softly. "I was just worried about you."

Deanne stared at her. Her mother continued. "I brought you an overnight case," she explained.

For the first time, Deanne saw the small blue leather suitcase. "I put some fresh clothes in it, and a toothbrush and hairbrush and some makeup. I thought you might like to freshen up."

Deanne felt foolish and grateful. "Thanks," she mumbled. She took the case from her mother. "I would like to do that. I'm sorry. Thank you."

Mrs. Vandervoort reached out and touched her daughter's cheek. "I'll be at home today," she said. "If you want or need anything . . . please call me."

Deanne nodded, fighting down a lump in her throat. "Thanks," she whispered again. Her mother sighed and left the room.

* * * * *

Deanne stood next to Matt's bed. She watched his pale face in the dim light of dusk. He didn't move. "Oh, Matt . . ." Deanne reached down and touched his cheek.

Then, she remembered something she learned as a VolunTeen. Even though a patient was asleep, he could still hear. It was a good idea to talk to a resting patient.

"I know you're going to get well," she began. "We have a date with Pam and Paul to play Scrabble Tuesday afternoon." Suddenly, she remembered that by Tuesday, she would be back in school. She put the thought out of her mind.

"Do you know, you've only beaten me four times?" she continued. "You've got to try again." She couldn't talk anymore. She reached down and took his hand. She held it tightly. "Hang on," she whispered. "Please, Matt, hang on!"

But he never moved. Deanne left his room and stepped back into the hall. She saw the Gleasons talking to each other.

"I think I'd better drive down to the lake and bring the kids back," Chuck Gleason said.

"Are—are you sure?" Janet asked. Her voice trembled.

"It's best that we're all here," he said. Janet nodded and hugged her husband. Deanne leaned against the wall for support.

* * * * *

The hospital chapel was small and quiet. Three wooden pews faced an altar where candles stood flickering. The chapel was universal. It was for people of all faiths.

Deanne sat next to Janet Gleason, staring at the glimmering candles. Janet held her hand. Outside, it was night again. But in the little room, time seemed suspended.

"You know," Janet said, half to herself. "Matt once told me that dying was just the last part of living, that a person couldn't die, unless he lived."

"He's not afraid," Deanne told her.

"I know," Janet responded. "He has great faith. He's never been afraid."

"But I am." Deanne whispered.

Janet squeezed her hand. "Me, too. But it's just because we'll miss him so much."

"I don't want him to die," Deanne said.

Tears filled her eyes. "I'll miss him so much."

"You made him very happy, Deanne," Janet said. "Thank you for that. Thank you for caring."

Deanne began to cry quietly. "I love him . . .," she sobbed. "I love him."

* * * * *

The rest of the Gleason family arrived. Anthony was half asleep, but they all stood around Matt's bed and spoke to him. Then they went and sat in the waiting room. Anthony fell asleep on the couch. Janette and Theresa played a game of cards. Tina and Deanne sat close together and talked. Chuck and Janet Gleason stayed in Matt's room. The night dragged on.

"Why are the nights so long?" Tina asked.

"I don't know," said Deanne. "Matt hates the nights, too." She rested her chin on her hand. "I sometimes sit by his bed and hold his hand until he falls asleep," she told Tina. "He loves to see the morning come. Every morning, when I go into his room, he says, 'Well, I made it through another night.' I used to get mad at him for being a pessimist. But now, I realize that he was really glad that the night was over. He loves the sunlight."

Suddenly, a red-haired nurse stuck her head in the waiting room. "Gleasons?" she asked. "Your parents want you to come to your brother's room."

Deanne's stomach lurched. Quickly, Tina woke up the sleeping Anthony. "Hurry," she said. They all went down the hall to Matt's room. Deanne stopped at the door. She couldn't go inside with the rest of them. The door closed quietly in her face.

She stood alone in the hall. She felt cold and numb. Her heart pounded. Her hands felt clammy. She walked to the end of the hall and stared at the closed blinds over the outside window. She stood there for a long time.

Deanne felt a gentle tug on her jeans leg. She looked down into Anthony's wide, tear-filled eyes.

"Matt went to sleep," the child said.

Her breath caught in her throat. She looked at Janet, who came up behind Anthony and put her arm around him. Bright tears filled Janet's eyes, but her face was peaceful and smiling.

"He just stopped breathing," she said. "Matt's at peace now. He doesn't hurt anymore."

Slowly, Deanne turned back to face the closed blinds. She felt empty. She reached up and absently opened the blind's slats. Outside, the first bright streaks of dawn were breaking through the gray cloud banks of the night.

She watched as the bright, golden ball of the sun broke over trees.

Thirteen

"Everybody's asking for you at the hospital, Deanne," Dr. Vandervoort said to his daughter as she sat hunched over her school books. She sat at the breakfast bar in their sunny kitchen.

Deanne looked up at his face, then glanced quickly away. "I've been very busy with my new classes and all," she shrugged.

"Too busy to stop by and say hello to everybody?"

"I'll go back sometime," she said quietly.

"You know, Pat Jacobson has a pile of VolunTeen service awards and certificates waiting for you in her office." He paused. "It's been a month, Deanne. You should start to think about the future."

"Five weeks and three days," Deanne said, closing her geometry book with a snap. "I can't go back. I hate that hospital. I never

117

want to go inside it again!"

Dr. Vandervoort tried a different tack. "That girl, Pam Miller. She stopped by my office yesterday to say good-bye." Deanne looked at him sharply. "She went home. She's in complete remission."

"I'm glad," Deanne said.

"Kids with cancer *do* get well, Deanne. She stopped by because she missed seeing you. She wanted me to know what a good friend you've been to her. She wanted to tell you goodbye herself."

"Dad, please!" Deanne cried, standing up while gathering her books. "I don't want to go back to the hospital."

As she started out the door toward her bedroom, he asked, "What shall I tell Mrs. Jacobson about your awards?"

"You could bring them home to me," Deanne said hopefully.

"No," he said simply. "I can't. If you want them, you'll have to go pick them up yourself."

"Then I don't want them," she said stubbornly. And she ran up the spiral staircase.

* * * * *

"Want some company?" Deanne heard

Susan's familiar voice.

"Sure," Deanne said, pushing her lunch tray aside. "You don't normally have this lunch period. Why today?"

Susan sighed. "I was helping Mrs. Wilson on a literature project, so I'm eating late today. So, how have you been? I haven't seen you much since school's started."

"Okay," Deanne said. "Classes are boring and I still can't stand the country club scene. I'm not doing much of anything."

"We miss you at the hospital," said Susan.

Deanne felt her defenses go up. "Mom's got me signed up for tennis lessons every Saturday morning . . .," she started.

"But you hate tennis," Susan said.

"It beats sitting around," said Deanne.

"You could come in on Saturdays. A few of us summer VolunTeens are working Saturdays and after school—"

"I don't want to," Deanne cut her off. "It was a fun thing to do this summer, but it was beginning to bore me."

Susan was silent for a minute. "Even Mrs. Sanders, the dragon lady, asked about you."

Deanne tried to look bored and uninterested. "She asked, 'Miss Pyle, whatever happened to Miss Vandervoort? Is she ill?' I said, 'No, Mrs. Sanders. She's too busy since school

119

started.' And she said, 'Funny, she didn't seem like a quitter.'"

Deanne's cheeks flushed hotly. "I'm not!" she cried. "Why can't everybody just leave me alone? I worked at the hospital for one whole summer. It was fun, but it's over. I don't ever want to go back there again!"

Then she picked up her tray and left the cafeteria.

* * * * *

Deanne lobbed the tennis ball absently against the net. It bounced back at her and she caught it. Already, the October mornings were chilly. The smell of autumn was in the air.

"Hey, Deanne. Need a partner?" She turned to face Judson Cortland. He was as blond and good-looking as ever.

"I was just thinking of giving up," she told him.

"Don't do that," he smiled. His teeth were white and even, his face still tanned. "Come on, let's hit a few," he urged. "Then, maybe, we can go get a soft drink."

"I'm supposed to meet Mom back at the Clubhouse," she explained.

"So? I'd still like to buy you a soft drink."

She paused and looked hard at him. "You don't have to be nice to me, Judson. Our mothers aren't around."

He cocked his head to one side and said, "Hey! No one's making me do anything. It's just that . . . well . . . I don't know. You've changed a lot over the summer."

She felt herself blushing. "How?" she asked. She enjoyed watching him squirm and grope for words.

"I don't know . . . you're just . . . different," he said shyly.

"I don't feel different," she said.

"Well, you are. Did something special happen this summer?" he asked.

"I did a lot of volunteer work at the hospital . . ." Her voice trailed off. "Look, I gotta go. Mom will be waiting."

"But, what about our game?" he asked. "And how about the pop?"

She called over her shoulder, "Thanks. Some other time." As she walked away she said to herself, Judson Cortland asked me out, unprompted by either of our mothers!

Six months before, it would have been the biggest moment in her life. Now, she couldn't have cared less.

* * * * *

The phone rang. It shattered the silence in the Vandervoort family room. Dr. Vandervoort answered it. He spoke quickly, then hung up.

"That was the hospital," he told Sylvia and Deanne. "One of my patients isn't doing well. I'm going to have to go in and examine him."

Mrs. Vandervoort put her needlepoint down. "Of course, dear," she smiled.

Deanne felt her pulse begin to race. She had an idea. "Dad," she started, "let me go with you. I want to get some of my things. This would be a perfect time."

"Oh, Hans," Mrs. Vandervoort interrupted. "It's already ten o'clock. You could be there for hours. Deanne, you can go anytime after school. Why now?"

"Please, Dad," Deanne said urgently. A special look passed between them.

"All right," he said. "But hurry up. I have to get going."

"I will," she called, running from the room to get her jacket and comb her hair.

They drove quickly to the hospital. "I don't know how long I'll be," he told her when they pulled into the parking lot.

"It's okay," she said. "I'm just going to clean out my locker. Then I'll go up to your office and wait. I can sleep on your couch."

"Like old times," he said.

"Almost," she said as they walked into the hospital together.

* * * * *

She didn't intend to go up to the Oncology floor. But, before she even realized it, she was there. The halls smelled of disinfectant and medication. They smelled familiar and sad.

"I won't go to his room!" she told herself firmly.

But, she was drawn there automatically. She passed the nurses' station. There wasn't anyone on duty that she knew.

She stood for a long time in front of room 438. Everything came back to her in a flood of memories. Tears sprang to her eyes. Her pain was real. Deanne sniffed and turned to go, when she heard the small, muffled crying of a child.

It was coming from behind that door, the one that she couldn't bare to touch. Slowly, Deanne reached out and pushed on the handle. It swung open easily.

A small form lay heaped in the one bed Deanne couldn't stand to look at. The night light glowed in the darkness. But, Deanne had to get closer in order to make out the huddled shape of a little girl.

"Hello," Deanne said. "Are you crying?"

"Who are you?" the girl asked. "Are you a nurse?"

"No," Deanne said. Before she could say anything else, the girl asked, "Are you an angel?"

"Oh, no," Deanne smiled. "I was walking down the hall and I heard you crying. What's wrong?"

"I'm scared," she said in her small voice.

"Why? Did you have a bad dream?"

"It's dark," said the child. "I'm scared in the dark. My mommy couldn't stay with me. I want to go home."

"Do you want me to get a nurse?" Deanne asked kindly.

"They're too busy. I'm a big girl. I'm almost six. I'm not supposed to be scared."

Deanne felt a lump rise up in her throat. She should turn and run away. She shouldn't stay. It was too painful for her.

She cleared her throat. "You know," she whispered. "I had a friend once . . . and he told me that when someone holds your hand it's easy to fall asleep. You won't ever be afraid as long as someone holds on."

"Where's your friend now?" the little girl asked.

"He, he had to go away."

"Will he come back?"

"No," Deanne murmured softly. Then she added, "But he's happy now." Deanne brushed the back of her hand across her eyes. "Why don't I pull up this chair and sit right next to your bed and hold your hand until you fall asleep?"

"Would you?" The child sounded relieved. "You won't leave?"

"Not until you're sound asleep. I promise," Deanne said.

The girl grasped Deanne's hand firmly and settled back on her pillow. Deanne held on tightly and leaned back in the chair. She knew the girl would be asleep in a few minutes.

Her eyes swept around the familiar room.

Everything was just as she remembered it. Except . . . except . . . "Good-bye, Matt." Deanne whispered into the darkness.

The familiar night sounds of the hospital settled in around her. The child's fingers slowly relaxed as she fell into a deep sleep. Deanne heard the child's rhythmic breathing. But Deanne didn't let go of her hand. For the first time in weeks she felt peaceful and content. She felt hopeful.

And she knew that she'd come home.

To become a hospital volunteer during the summer, after school and/or on weekends, call the Volunteer Program Director at your local hospital.

ABOUT THE AUTHOR

Lurlene McDaniel lives in Chattanooga, Tennessee, and is a favorite author of young people all over the country. Her best-selling books about kids overcoming problems such as cancer, diabetes, and the death of a parent or sibling draw a wide response from her readers. Lurlene says that the best compliment she can receive is having a reader tell her, "Your story was so interesting that I couldn't put it down!" To Lurlene, the most important thing is writing an uplifting story that helps the reader to look at life from a different perspective.

Six Months to Live, the first of the best-selling books about Dawn Rochelle and her courageous fight against cancer, was placed in a time capsule at the Library of Congress in Washington, D.C. The capsule is scheduled to be opened in the year 2089.

Other Willowisp Press books by Lurlene McDaniel include *I Want to Live*, *Mother, Please Don't Die*, and *Sometimes Love Just Isn't Enough*.